# Life
# Beyond
# Us

## An eclectic journey through the afterlife

By Jennifer A. Bryant

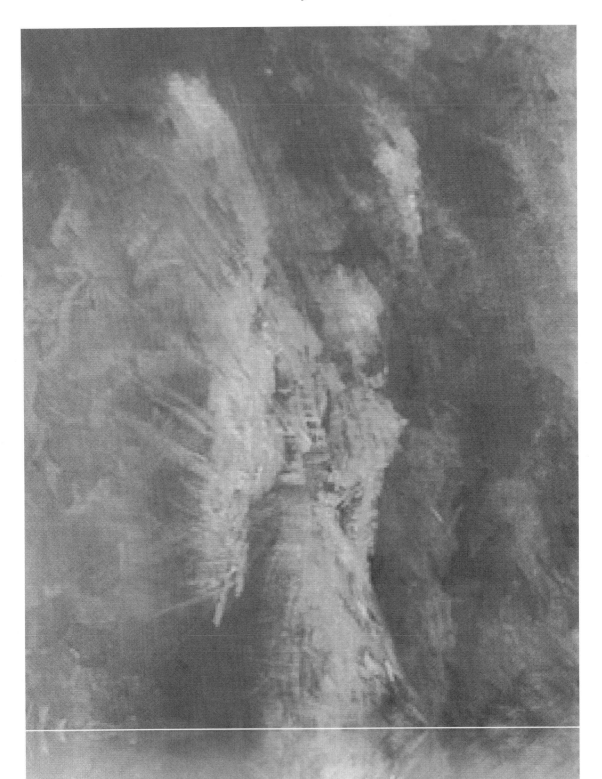

Artist - P. Stevenson

Copyright © 2021 Jennifer Bryant

All rights reserved.

ISBN:978-1-7372790-2-0

Breath of Spirit Publishing

# Dedications

I dedicate this book to All beings of the Great Beyond, who guide us to the greatest mysteries and divine sources.

I offer up my love and most profound gratitude to the Spirits mentioned in this book which bring the wisdom of the afterlife to light.

Through their presence, we can learn more about the divine mysteries, life, ourselves, and our soul's purpose.

I am blessed to have been by the side of so many people and animals during their times of cross-over.

In honor, I share their love, inspiring wisdom, and magnificent guidance so we may experience the spiritual life that exists beyond us.

I extend special gratitude to my friends, Artist Patti Stevenson and Copyeditor Polly Stephenson, for devoting their time, talent, and love to help me complete this book.

Just because we have been told the world exists

a certain way, that doesn't mean it does.

## Introduction

As a metaphysical practitioner, I utilize a vast spectrum of spiritual communications, which took years of spirit training to master. I emphasize *spirit training* because, as you will see, spirit ensured I had no other choice but *to learn.*

"Life Beyond Us" shares my personal journey of awakening to the signs, mysteries, and communications of the afterlife. I now share those extraordinary times with you, hoping you will recognize the blessing of spiritual guidance within your own life.

The mind-bending chapters of my life experiences harmonize the readers with extra-sensory abilities allowing them to go beyond the self to see, hear, and feel the spirit world.

This mystical journey begins with odd knowings during my childhood experiences. As time unfolds, awe-inspiring, mind-blowing experiences clearly reveal that we *can, and should,* continue our relationships with loved ones, pets, and divine beings on the other side.

The Spirits mentioned in this book make sure we know they are still very much alive!

Each chapter is filled with a symphony of inspiring, amazing, miraculous, strange, and even hair-raising subjects that bring the reader to thought-provoking heights that speak to the heart and soul.

Spirit, whether your God Source, angels, aliens, loved ones, pets, or the butterfly who flew past you, are all family because we are all of the divine first being or beginning.

The experiences shared in "Life Beyond Us" remind us that no one, whether in body or spirit, is ever alone.

All our relations and even those we don't know are fully alive, guiding us in every moment to become the person our soul already knows we are.

With the help of the many spirit guides mentioned here, we can now witness the awe and wonder of the invisible worlds in action. And, let me say too, that I am *so glad* I had witnesses to these events!

I leave each story open to the imagination because each experience carries its own message and point for each reader. I don't ask you to believe anything I share. I do hope you come to know that your loved ones in spirit and all beings are alive and accessible and that you enjoy their presence.

We never truly know the value of an experience until it becomes a memory. May the memories shared here awaken you to the love that exists in the *Life Beyond Us.*

# Contents

| | Page |
|---|---|
| **Chapter 1 - The Initiations** | 19 |
| A Rattlesnake's Energy | 20 |
| Bull Headed | 22 |
| Knowing to Look | 23 |
| Suicide Sight | 24 |
| Ladder Man | 25 |
| In a New York Minute | 26 |
| My Angel Boy | 29 |
| Helping the Neighbor | 31 |
| It's Momma's Turn | 32 |
| Cross and Staff | 38 |
| Michael Shines | 40 |
| No Pain, No Gain | 41 |
| Untouchable | 44 |
| No Vitals | 47 |

## Chapter 2 - The Signs     48

Bells     49

Candy Bars     50

Children Know     51

Beyond Texting     52

He Peeps In     53

A Pearl of Wisdom     54

You Are My Sunshine     56

Gettin' Er' Done     58

Sister Love     60

Get Him Out of my Bed     61

Spirit Maintenance     62

Hotel Girl     63

Destined Love     64

Soul to Soul     65

A Bright Light Shines     69

| | |
|---|---|
| Chapter 3 - The Mysteries | 71 |
| Spirit Bubbles | 72 |
| True Prayer | 73 |
| Watching George | 75 |
| I'm Here | 76 |
| Sky Beings | 77 |
| Tower Man | 80 |
| Creatures and Bugs | 81 |
| Prayed Up | 84 |
| Shadow Man | 85 |
| Little Timmy | 86 |
| Roping Creature | 88 |
| Clicking Beings | 89 |
| We're Back | 92 |
| Money Game | 93 |
| Damn That's Good | 94 |
| Witches and Invisible Cars | 96 |
| Lance and Cooper | 100 |

## Chapter 4 - Two Years of Darkness — 103

| | |
|---|---|
| Head's Up | 106 |
| Midnight Quiet | 107 |
| Black Dust | 109 |
| Devil's Den | 110 |
| Soul Flames | 112 |
| Lord's Prayer | 113 |
| Holy Fire Towel | 115 |
| Alcohol Death Grip | 117 |
| Smoke and Mirrors | 119 |
| Mountain Man | 120 |
| Electrocution Sign | 122 |
| Lightning Strikes Twice | 123 |

## Chapter 5 - The Communications — 126

| | |
|---|---|
| The Mentalist | 127 |
| Crash | 130 |
| I'm Busy | 131 |
| Finger Hold | 133 |
| Artists Live Too | 134 |
| His Rhapsody | 136 |
| Dad's Call into the Light | 139 |
| The Death Tree | 142 |

| | |
|---|---|
| Not Blessing me | 146 |
| Vaccine Sign | 148 |
| The Spiritually Abled | 149 |
| Phoenix Rising | 151 |
| Sensing The Time | 155 |
| Remote Views | 157 |
| A Glorious New Life | 159 |
| **Chapter 6 - The Guidance** | **168** |
| Nine Mom Signs | 169 |
| Raiding the Frig | 174 |
| A Creative Viewing | 175 |
| Last Birthday Card | 176 |
| Her Scent | 178 |
| Still Dancing and Walking | 179 |
| Helpful | 181 |
| Motherly Guidance | 182 |
| The Eye of Ma | 183 |
| My Heartbeat | 185 |
| Lighting it Up | 186 |
| Mom's Mystical Girl | 188 |
| Heads Up | 189 |

## Chapter 7 - The Preparation — 190

Hoodjie-woodjie and the Light — 192

Happy Me up — 195

Checks and Lavender — 197

In Eden — 198

Sacrifice — 199

Little Reaper — 202

Something Better — 204

Out-of-Body — 205

The Calling Stone — 206

Shiny Calling Cards — 208

Angel Bear — 210

The Other You — 212

Signs of Home — 214

A Mouthful of Leaving — 216

Tasty Jen — 219

Knock, Knock — 220

The Code — 221

Sweet Potato Soufflé — 223

| | |
|---|---|
| Chapter 8 - Animal Spirit Guides | 224 |
| Heartbeat of Home | 226 |
| Animal Talk | 228 |
| Shakers | 229 |
| Kitten Love | 231 |
| Raccoon Tears | 232 |
| Mr. Furb | 235 |
| The Flower | 238 |
| Far Away | 239 |
| Ms. Furb | 240 |
| Meshach | 242 |
| Noble Hawk | 243 |
| Siwee | 244 |
| Maple and Champers | 246 |
| Invisible Friends | 248 |
| Pup prayer | 250 |
| No Time | 251 |
| Dakota | 253 |
| A Brother Knows | 256 |
| Our Agreement | 258 |
| Dying Together | 260 |

| | |
|---|---|
| Cat Box! | 262 |
| Helping Brother | 263 |
| A Gift for Momma | 264 |
| Snoopy Dance | 265 |
| New Colors | 266 |
| The Mysterious Voice | 267 |
| I Know My Way | 269 |
| Two for One | 270 |
| Karma and Dharma | 271 |
| Angels Are Sweet | 272 |
| Afterlife Thoughts | 274 |
| Spirit Word Search | 277 |

**Please Note** - Names have been changed to protect privacy. While religious terminology is used throughout "Life Beyond Us," the information shared is through experiences not related to any branch of organized religion or any system of religious beliefs.

Before my journey in service became recognized as a natural wellness practitioner and metaphysical channel, I worked as a hair designer, dedicated my life to my son, and lived a life of mysterious experiences.

My first memory of writing began as a child. Born and raised on a farm in Georgia, I adored nature and animals more than anything else. I would often slip off to quiet places to draw or write poetry about upsetting experiences people endured. I learned quickly that I understood the language of nature and animals better than human language.

Born hell-bent on freedom from my first breath, I began incorporating self-empowerment into my writings in my teen years. At the age of thirteen, having witnessed much heartache and trauma that people inflict upon others, I started writing poetry for those who were suffering as a creative way to help them feel better.

Being a natural farm girl so connected with nature and animals, freedom and comfort was all I ever wanted to return to. As a fiercely independent teen, I would not be restrained by humans' rules, which led me to live out my teen years first with my aunt, a runaway shelter, and then with my gramma.

While I wanted to work in a job supporting my passion for nature and animals - life, as it does so perfectly, paved the way. I first pursued the corporate world, then cosmetology. I married at the age of nineteen and gave birth to my darling son at the age of twenty-one.

Years later, an explosion of life challenges took place in my life. After experiencing a whirlwind of upset when my son and I had medical issues, both of my grandmothers and my dad passed away, back to back - my soul called out.

Something sparked within me. On a wing and a prayer, I took a leap based solely on faith. I divorced my husband, closed my salon, packed my belongings, grabbed my son, put the pets in the car, and left to begin a new life.

Leaving my family and all I knew behind, I moved to the top of a mountain where I knew no one except nature and animals. I opened my salon, and our new life set itself instantaneously.

Having my son by my side, our days were filled with love and joy, volunteering, rehabilitating local wildlife, hiking, and enjoying outdoor activities. We truly enjoyed the diverse, wholesome environments mountain life offered us. I, the child who began life understanding the language of nature and animals better than humans, was home.

As life does what it does, ultimately manifesting what is best for us, the stage was set for my next call to action, which turned out to be the catalyst to reawakening my soul's living purpose.

Through a near-death, out-of-body, life-changing experience, new channels opened and led me through a rigorous, ten-year cleansing and ascension process. Once again, all I knew ended, and another new life began.

I traversed many years of mind-blowing experiences during my reawakening, which also helped me master my extra-sensory abilities. This, too, had its ups, downs, and curveballs. However, I eventually realized that my experiences were everyone's experiences, and the knowledge would somehow be used in good service to benefit all life.

I strapped in and moved through the unknown and miraculous experiences trusting that the outcome of every experience would be more miraculous than the challenge. And, it was.

My salon chair has always been a catalyst for people feeling comfortable enough to spill their hearts out freely. I have spent thirty years listening to people share their trauma, challenges, heartfelt stories, joys, and pains.

Having had so many challenging experiences myself, I noticed when I shared my experiences and outside-the-box insights, it magically transformed others' sufferings and worries into empowerment and peace.

My living purpose became clear. I was to share my experiences and reveal the divine light driving each experience. Being a natural-born underdog and make-it-better girl, I took pen to paper and revealed just that. Through my life and writings, others can enjoy an intimate journey through themselves and reawaken to the elixir of the Spirit.

For the little girl who began life loving nature, animals, and writing to help others feel better, I hope my life experiences bring forth the great mysteries of the spirit world so you, too, may enjoy the miracles of what awaits in the *Life Beyond Us*.

Humans may "tell" you life is a certain way

But life "teaches" you - *it is not.*

# Chapter One

# The Initiations

A bird does not sing because it has something to say.
It sings because it has a beautiful song
to share with the world.

My eclectic journey with the beyond began with early childhood experiences, which led me to conclude there was much more to life than what I could see.

My first memorable childhood experience began with the spirit of a Rattlesnake.

## A Rattlesnake's Energy

I was around seven years old when my life was spared by a simple feeling my dad had. I went outside to go feed the farm animals, which was my favorite thing to do.

As I went to pick up a feed bucket that was turned upside down, my dad stepped onto the porch and yelled out, *"Jennifer, don't touch that bucket!"*

Well, I, the stubborn child I was, looked over at him with my nasty eye and said, *"Why? I want to feed the animals!"*

As I continued reaching for the bucket, he came barreling off the porch toward me, yelling, *"If you touch that bucket, I'm gonna bust your ass! Get in the house right now!"*

Of course, I was mad and pouted as I walked away. Then, something made me stop and look back at him. Just as I did, I watched him lift the bucket, and a rattlesnake jumped out and bit him on the wrist. He quickly grabbed me by the arm, and we ran into the house.

As I watched him slit his wrist with a knife to drain the poison, I wondered how he *knew* to stop me. Had the snake bitten me, I would have been dead in seconds.

My dad often seemed to *know* things before they happened, but I wondered how he knew enough to stop me from picking up the bucket, but not for himself.

While he obviously saved my life, I knew something too. I knew that if I had picked up that bucket, the snake would not have bitten me. I knew it would have felt my love for animals and would have stayed calm.

I understood the snake had bitten my dad because he was angry, and his nervous energy scared the snake. He also hunted animals, and I knew the animals knew that about him.

I still believe this today and continue to use the energy of love and honor when communicating with animals.

The next mysterious sign I recall was also around the age of seven.

## Bull Headed

My family and I were going to visit a neighbor one day. My dad decided to take a shortcut through a Brahma bull pasture, and our car broke down in the middle of the field.

We started walking to the neighbor's house. All of a sudden, my dad told us to stop walking and freeze in place.

We were standing right in the middle of the field with the biggest bull I had ever seen, staring us down. My dad was afraid the bull would charge us.

He said, *"When I tell you to run, everyone better run."* Of course, he looked at me with his disciplining eye.

I remember locking eyes with the bull just gazing into his eyes. I could feel he was looking into my eyes too. I spoke to the bull in my head, and I knew he heard me.

I felt a connection with him and thought to myself, *"Pfft, dad is wrong. That bull isn't going to hurt us. He's just curious."*

Well, dad yelled, *"Run!"* Everyone ran, of course, except me. I just kept looking into the bull's eyes and began walking backward.

Even with all the running and yelling from my family, I stayed connected with the bull. He never even moved a muscle. To my child-mind, it was as if the bull knew me.

Of course, once home, I was in trouble with my dad, but it was worth it to have connected with such a beautiful massive creature.

## Knowing to Look

When I was around the same age, a tornado hit our town. Our barn was down, and our horses had run off. Dad put all of us in the car, and we went searching for the horses. We finally found them at a neighbors house.

Dad tethered the two horses to the back of the car while my Mom rode on one of them. On the ride home, I was in the backseat messing with my brothers. After a few minutes of driving, I remember the air felt strange, and a weird silence hit my ears.

Again, I *knew* something. So I jumped up and looked out the back window at my Mom. She wasn't there. I yelled, *"Daddy, stop. Mom is gone!"*

He slammed on the brakes and jumped out of the car to find my Mom nearly lifeless, lying on the ground.

The horses had knocked her off and trampled her when they began fighting. Mom had severe injuries and was laid up for a long time, but she survived.

A few days later, I was outside, sitting in the strawberry field, thinking how happy I was that my Mom was alive. I knew had I not looked for her at the exact moment I did, she would have died.

I wondered how this stuff happens, and always at the perfect time to save people's lives?

This day in the strawberry field was when I first began meditating with nature, animals, the sky, and the unknown.

Then around the age of nine, I experienced a whole new level of awareness outside my comfort zone.

## Suicide Sight

My family was vacationing in the Florida keys on our annual lobstering trip.

My parents had a fight, and my dad took the car and drove four hours back home, leaving us there. Luckily, my aunt was there with us to bring us home.

When we returned to town, my Mom took us to my Gramma's house. She refused to go back to the house with my dad until things settled down.

I was playing quietly when suddenly I felt sick to my stomach. Then, out of nowhere, like watching a movie, I had a vision of my dad. He was drunk. I saw a scene with a lot of guns lying around, and I knew he was going to kill himself.

I didn't say anything to anyone because things were bad enough. A few minutes later, the phone rang. I knew it was my dad.

He was drunk and told my Mom if she didn't get us all back home, he would blow his head off. We ended up going home.

When we arrived, there were a lot of policemen inside. When I walked through the door, I saw my dad sitting on the couch with his guns laid out all around him.

He was holding a gun to his head, threatening to kill himself.

Eventually, the policemen calmed him down, and quiet followed. I wondered for weeks *how I could see a vision like that and have it come true - when I wasn't even there.*

At that time, my young mind reasoned that *there must be something wrong with me.*

## Ladder Man

This experience happened around the age of fifteen. I lived with my Gramma.

One day, as I was cleaning the house, I happened to look out the window at the neighbor's house. I saw an old man stepping down from a ladder. I wasn't really paying much attention, but I did notice he disappeared quickly.

The house had been for sale and vacant for a long time. I assumed someone had purchased the home, and the man was just outside doing repairs.

Later that evening, Gramma and I were having dinner. I asked her who bought the house next door."

She said, *"No one, why?"*

With confusion, I said, *"Well, there was an old man out there on a ladder today. I kept looking for him to say Hi, but then he and the ladder were gone."*

I told her what he was wearing and what he looked like. Then, I took her to the window to show her where I had seen him. She sat back down at the table with a funny smile.

She then said, *"Oh, that's the man who used to own the house. He was painting the house, fell off the ladder, and died a while back. He died in the exact spot you showed me. That is why the house is on the market."*

I was stunned she was so nonchalant about it and a little creeped out that I could now see *dead people.*

But, Ladder man proved to me that there really is a rarely seen invisible world happening right in front of us.

## In A New York Minute

This next experience was pivotal and laid the path for my future works in service.

My friend's parents were psychic detectives for various New York police departments. They used their extra-sensory abilities in good service by finding missing children.

I spent a weekend with them at their house, which was a 100+ year-old hotel they made into their home. I was already completely intrigued and fascinated with my friend's parents' unique abilities and life work.

Still, when I learned her dad was a clairvoyant, remote viewer and performed seances and exorcisms, *I was like a moth to light.*

I asked him a million questions about the spirit world, and he graciously shared his wisdom with me. The only subjects he would not discuss with me were exorcisms and the dark dimensions.

He made it clear those works were not for me and told me to not get involved in those areas. I had a feeling he could see my future, and his message was, in some way, guidance. I wondered how he could do that but gave it no more thought because I trusted him.

Later, my friend and I went horseback riding after a heavy snowfall. As I jumped down off the horse, my foot went into a hole, and my knee popped. I had re-torn a previous tendon injury in my knee and couldn't walk.

Her dad retrieved me and brought me back to the house.

He meditated on my injury and then reached into his spiritual medicine cabinet, which had all sorts of herbal concoctions he had made.

He pulled out a balm and applied it to my knee. I could tell he was working with *something or someone* other than himself as he held his hand over my knee. I didn't know what he was doing, but I could feel heat coming from the palm of his hand. He said, *"You will be fine now."*

The pain had magically disappeared. I was so fascinated by his spiritual doctoring ability, I knew right then I wanted to help people and spirits beyond us like he did.

Later that evening, I could not fall asleep at bedtime due to the gathering of people my friend's dad had over. I heard people making noise, talking, walking, laughing, and carrying on conversations.

I thought they must be some pretty interesting people if they knew him. I asked my friend if her dad's friends were psychics and if we could go downstairs and meet them.

She laughed and said, *"Oh, no. There's no one here. Those are the hotel spirits and the souls my dad has worked with. They carry on every weekend."* Well, I was so excited. I stayed up half the night listening to them with pure awe.

After returning home, I felt something about me had changed. I *knew* something changed when I quickly lost contact with my friend. Even though I went to school with her and saw her every day, she simply disappeared.

I could no longer remember her name, her parents' names, what any of them looked like, or even the town they lived in. It was as if it had all been *erased*.

I could only recall the house, my experiences, and what I felt inside. It's as if the people never existed.

Now, having years of experience learning about the spirit world, I know I didn't spend the weekend with them for the physical relationship. I was there to receive an initiation, what I now understand as a *spiritual download.*

The result of this experience made me want to seek a personal relationship with the invisible world and be in spiritual service. And, so I did.

In a New York minute, I was hooked and obviously for a divinely manifested reason. Turns out, now, 37 years later, I and my life's work is just like my friend's dad. Of course, just as he guided me, *minus the seances and exorcisms.*


The next sign from the spirit world hit the depths of my heart through my son.

## My Angel Boy

My son and I were decorating for the Christmas season when he was only two or three years old.

I told him he could unpack the boxes but not plug any lights into the wall socket. I went into a closet to get a box while my son stood outside, unpacking things.

Suddenly, I felt an eerie silence fill the air and called out to him. He didn't answer. I ran out of the closet and thought I would die when I saw my son lying motionless on the floor.

Noticing Christmas lights plugged into an electrical socket, I knew he had been electrocuted.

I picked him up from the floor and put him on the couch in a hysterical panic, screaming for him to wake up. He finally began to come to a foggy awareness.

As he did, he said, *"Mommy, look at the big, pretty light."*

Hearing those words, I freaked and yelled loudly, *"Stay away from the light! Don't look at the light!"*

He then smiled and said he saw three pretty lights, *"Three light people,"* as he called them. I knew he was seeing three angels because I saw them myself in my mind's eye.

I went numb and calmly said, *"Don't look at the angels! Stay here with Mommy."*

I knew that once my son was in their presence, I was no longer in charge of his life. I just stood there repeatedly, asking the angels not to take him. My son, groggy and confused, then opened his eyes.

After thanking God repeatedly and checking him over like a madwoman, I rushed my son to the doctor to have him examined.

He was perfectly fine. However, the doctor informed me that he might have electrical issues with his heart later in life, but it should balance out over time. As it happened, he did have troublesome heart issues in his teen years, but they eventually disappeared.

Once I had calmed down from the thought of losing my precious son, I pondered the harrowing event so deeply that I felt something inside me click.

I knew right then I, as his Mom, was *secondary*; the three angels have been and would continue to be his main life guides.

It is through this experience I came to know, without a doubt, that divine beings exist. This was also the very moment, out of pure gratitude, that I gave myself to the divine mystery.

From that moment on, I called my son "My Angel" because his experience with the divine, in many ways, saved me from myself.

## Helping the Neighbor

After my son's electrocution, I noticed little signs that he had some extra-sensory ability going on.

He had a keen sense of seeing through people and their truth, and at times, he could see what others did not.

My son loved helping our neighbor, John, work outside doing house chores. One day, my son and I were outside, and he looked over at our neighbors' house and waived.

He said, *"Hi, John!"*

Then he turned to me and said, *"Mommy, can I go help, John?"*

Well, I looked over out of pure curiosity. I knew John wasn't outside.

John had recently passed away. However, my son saw him, plain as day.

## It's Momma's Turn

Thirteen years after my son's out-of-body, near-death experience, I had my own.

I was at a point where I realized my life was not in a good place. I was fed up and angry at myself for making un-beneficial choices.

Driving to work one morning while feeling this intense anger, I said to myself, *"I'm not going to live this way anymore."* Disgust welled up inside of me, and out of the blue and I burst into prayer.

A passion came from deep within me as the words flew out of my mouth demanding change. I didn't ask God to fix my life. I told God to fix it.

Those of you who know me are aware I can be a little feisty. And I certainly was in that moment. I prayed aloud, fiercely telling God, *"You had better get down here now and fix my life now or just take me home. I have screwed it up, and I can't fix it myself. I'm done! I don't want to live this way anymore!"*

Little did I know how quickly the divine would respond.

I arrived at work and routinely continued with my day. I had even forgotten all about my morning hissy-fit prayer. Around lunchtime, I decided to go to the bank. Driving there, not three hours after my passionate prayer, a vision began to unfold like a movie in my mind's eye.

It all happened so fast. I saw a white car coming toward me and hit me head-on. I thought, What a strange vision!

Just as the vision faded away, I looked ahead and actually saw a white car coming toward me. It crossed the yellow line.

I knew it was going to hit me head-on. In a second's time, I recall thinking three things simultaneously:

*Oh, no! This isn't what I meant...*

*Ah, sh\*t, this is gonna hurt...*

*Well, I guess my prayer's been answered.*

In that moment, I was positive God chose to take my life rather than fix it.

Then I panicked and thought, No, I can't leave my son behind! My son was the only thing I wanted to live for. Yet, at the same time, I knew whatever was happening was sealed.

I was then drawn to look upward to my left. I saw a huge, brilliant being of light descending toward me at hyper speed. I knew this being was Archangel Michael.

Michael's energy force pull me out of my body - and my car. Floating in a vortex of cloud-like, dark, silent space, I could only see a trail of light emanating from Michael's path ahead of me. I was magnetically connected to it. I gently glided upward behind Michael, having no movement or control of my own.

I then heard the cars crash behind me. I instantly realized Michael had taken me out of my body long before the crash even took place. I knew the body I left behind felt the impact of the hit, but I felt nothing but perfection.

When I began to turn my head to look at the crash scene, Michael halted me and kept my gaze on him instead. I felt I didn't need to see the crash.

At that moment, I realized I was no longer alive on Earth. I felt a heaviness move through me when I realized I had left my son behind. I thought, *No, I can't die. I must stay for him.*

Michael then reminded me of the day he had been electrocuted and that he is always watched over. Understanding that Michael was one of the three angels that had visited my son, I thought, *Okay, then. I'm ready to go.*

I looked forward into Michael's trail of light with awe and was bathed in the illumination. As we went higher, a whitish haze began to appear all around me. It was so silent, peaceful, pure, and complete.

There was no emotion, thought, or separation. Telepathic knowing took the place of spoken language, and I was unified with everything, everywhere, completely immersed in love.

As I gazed at Michael ahead of me, the light trail began to expand, and I merged deeper into it. Then I began to hear a faint, angelic, divine sound. It wasn't music, yet it was the most magical symphony of immaculate sound. I remembered knowing that sound.

Then, the white haze became thicker, and we picked up speed. As we began to lean toward the right, I saw a piercing, brilliant white light beginning to engulf everything. The bright light exploded as we entered it.

I was then standing inside a whitish space in front of an entryway. Archangel Michael was to my left, and Archangel Gabriel was to my right. Neither, by the way, were like humans, nor were they male or female. They were just illuminated beings, both masculine and feminine.

I knew them well, and they knew me *perfectly*. I sensed this was not the first time we had been together. Michael and Gabriel knew everything about my being, as evidenced when we then exchanged telepathic conversation.

While I don't recall what the angels said to me, I do recall what I said to them. They must have told me I would be going back to Earth because I remember my *adamant* disagreement. I fought, telling them I didn't want to go back.

Then they both spoke something to me, and whatever they said led me to look ahead into the entryway.

The entry was dark. I had a sliver of lingering perception about how humans say the darkness is a bad thing. I remember thinking, *Um, that's pretty dark in there, and* questioned if they were going to send me in there.

Then I came to know why the entryway looked dark. The light inside was so bright and blinding it appeared black. *As I* curiously peered into the void of nothingness, I felt a massive compelling force coming forth.

I began to feel the space itself morph into something. It became like gentle water moving in waves. Then the waves began to shape themselves into an illuminated, fluid-like being floated *as* the air.

As the being approached the entryway where I stood, I and *everything* became silent and awe-filled.

I knew this being was beyond perfection. I knew I had been with this being before. I knew its presence. It was The Source of All - the omnipresent being we people refer to as God, Creator.

I knew I was to refer to this being as "The Source" instead of the name *God* and why. The word God was only to be spoken in specific dimensions.

I immediately opened my arms wide, kneeled, and bowed. Source God sent through me what I can only describe as a loving smile, saying, *"Nay. Stand, stand. All are equal."*

Simultaneously, Source God's power lifted me to an upright standing position, directly facing Its presence. I say *It* because referring to God as male or female would completely defile the perfect beingness God is.

Communication with Source God was telepathic and much different from the communication with Michael and Gabriel. The language of Source God was instantly understood and more accessible.

I knew without a doubt this magnificent being had dealt with me before at this very entryway, yet in a different way. I knew everything and also nothing at the same time.

I, of course, was no longer feisty. Now, I lovingly expressed my desire to stay in the afterlife. Source God's fluid presence began to move closer toward me. As it did, slow motion took place, and I began to sense a spinning motion around me.

There was a deafening silence, but at the same time, I could hear the sacred music echoing everywhere. Source God then spoke and filled me up with endless wisdom.

Source God stretched out an image of what could only be described in human terms as an illuminated arm. I thought, *Oh, good, I'm going to get a hug and be granted to stay.*

As Source God reached toward me, I saw its light move toward my chest. In a flash, a brilliant, blinding light exploded.

I flung backward as I stretched out my arms, saying, "*No!*"

The next thing I recall is being enveloped in a white, hazy cloud. At first, I thought I was sent to another place in the afterlife. The white haze around me looked just like the heavenly space where I had just been. I also still felt the same way.

I then realized I was sitting inside my vehicle, and the white haze was simply the contents of my car's airbag.

Still not believing God sent me back, I began to question whether I was alive or dead. I felt like I was dead, or at least still floating in heaven.

Perhaps, I thought, I had been sent back as a spirit guide, and I was therefore just hovering in the car. I could still feel Michael nearby helping me understand, so I just waited.

However, when a friend stopped to help me get out of my car, I knew I was back in my body. I sat there shaking my head, stunned they sent me back. But, I felt so perfect. I couldn't give thought to anything less than that.

Michael then sent his wisdom through me. I knew that my prayer had been answered, and neither I nor my life would ever be the same. *And it wasn't. It gave birth to my soul's living purpose, which is reflected in all of my writings.*

I have a beautiful daily reminder imprinted on my forearm from the burn of the airbag chemicals. It's the shape of Archangel Michael flying upward, exactly as I experienced him.

Interestingly, as one of my editors suggested, I went through this book and changed all the references of the word "Source God" to "God Source."

That evening during meditation, I received a transmission from my communications guide, Archangel Gabriel, to not change any words in the book. I woke the following day to continue editing the book only to find the changes I made the day before were gone. All references to "God Source" were changed back to *"Source God."*

*Just a magical reminder that the divine tends to everything perfectly and as it should be.*

## Cross and Staff

Not long after returning from the afterlife, I experienced a few awe-inspiring, mysterious events.

One of these miraculous moments involved a cross charm my son had given me. I wore this cross on my necklace and cherished it deeply because, for me, it symbolized my son's moment in the light with the angels.

When my car accident occurred, the cross ended up acting as a barrier. It had blocked a hard object from impaling my heart.

When the object hit the cross, it hit so hard it mangled the charm into the shape of a rod-like staff. Now the cross, having saved my life, held even more meaning. I shared this angelic life-saving experience with everyone I could to reveal the miracle of spirit.

One day, I was sharing my story with a client, and when I grabbed my necklace to show her the staff-cross, it was gone. I was heartbroken it was missing.

Now, I had that charm attached with a triple-loop fastener that had to be spiraled three times, using pliers, to get it onto my necklace in the first place. Baffled by its disappearance, I searched everywhere for hours, but the staff-cross was nowhere to be found.

Finally, I accepted that spirit must have removed it for a reason.

I knew I didn't need an object to honor the divine because they were clearly active in my life. So, I let it go.

Well, the next day, I opened the door at work, and there lay my staff-cross on the floor at my feet!

I nearly fell to my knees in amazement.

When I went to pick it up, I understood what a miracle really means. I saw that my once-mangled staff-cross had been unbent and reshaped into a perfect cross again! Strangely, the fastener had also been removed.

I proudly put the cross back on my necklace, and it didn't leave my neck again until eight years later - when I entered the second phase of my two years of darkness.

Then, my cross once again disappeared at my boyfriend's house. I never found it again, *and I didn't need to.*

## Michael Shines

Not long after my near-death, out-of-body experience, I was lying restless in bed one night, trying my best to fall asleep.

When I finally got comfortable, I heard an extremely high-pitched sound and mysteriously went deaf. A strange silence I had never experienced before filled my bedroom.

My eyes were closed, seeing only darkness until an extremely bright light lit up my vision. I immediately opened my eyes and gasped when I saw a tremendous, glorious being of light hovering at the foot of my bed.

The being gently waved like illuminated rippling water as it looked down upon me.

At first, I was a little frightened. However, when I noticed my dogs were calmly lying down, paws crossed, looking lovingly at the light being, peace and awe came over me.

Through dead silence, the being then spoke, saying, *"I am Archangel Michael."* Total and complete love filled me in that moment.

Michael hovered for a few seconds, then slowly faded away, leaving only tiny flickering lights in the air before complete darkness enveloped the room once again.

I fell asleep as if I had been sprinkled with slumber-inducing angel dust.

I awoke the next morning knowing Michael appeared so I could connect easier with his presence and communications. And it definitely worked!

## No Pain, No Gain

When I *"came to"* inside my wrecked car after returning from the light, I felt no pain at all. Past that moment, I saw everything through the eyes of a child.

There was nothing wrong with me, other people, the world, or anything else. Everything was pure and perfect. I also had the uncanny ability to reveal the divine aspects in any given negative situation. So much so that my friend nicknamed me *Glossy*.

People began commenting about physical things about my body from the accident that I had not noticed. My son discovered that one of my toes was broken, and one client noticed my nose was twisted and fractured.

Another client pointed out a large cyst on my neck and airbag burns on my arms - *none of which did I ever see with my own eyes.*

I honestly began to question whether I was alive in body or just a spirit. This was a valid thought because my friends and physicians often asked me the same thing.

I figured, *"Well, I'm here in some form, and I have scissors in my hand every day, so maybe I should get rebalanced into this world."*

I called my friend, a Healing Touch practitioner, and asked if she would help realign my energy field. When I sat in her chair, she felt my energy field and said it had been jolted to the far right of my body.

She asked if I wanted her to put it back in alignment. I said, *"Well, I have to function here, so I guess so."* - Worst decision ever!

When she finished realigning my energy field, a tremendous rush of pain shot throughout my body, and I felt my mind shift. I instantly realized what I had done and begged her to put my energy field back where it was.

She, of course, said, *"I can't do that."*

I was so angry. I went as far as asking her, *"If I drive my car into a mountain, will that pop it out again?"*

That's how desperate I was to get my glorious child-heart feeling back.

She said, *"You can't do that, Jennifer."*

I knew I couldn't, but the idea was a worthy one. I was so upset with myself. I had just defiled the most amazing, divine gift of spiritual perfection that Michael, Gabriel, and God had blessed me with. But it was already done.

I was clearly aware that spirit governs me and my actions, so I felt this moment was supposed to happen.

Later, I understood this realignment had to take place so I could better serve my living purpose as a holistic, metaphysical guide.

In order to know the metamorphosis of the soul's human experience *(beginning, middle, and end)* within and beyond time and space, I had to experience it.

## Untouchable

I had multiple extra-sensory abilities rising to the surface at lightning speed. However, I had no idea what to do with the abilities or even what to think about them.

Like many people, I was taught by religion and condemning people that extra-sensory abilities were evil and witchy. *Thankfully, a trip into the light of the afterlife nullifies anything mankind teaches.*

I knew I would use my heightened sensory skills to be in good service, but I was having difficulty understanding them.

As guided, I was led to a woman who had experienced the same as I. She had already been there, done that, and had mastered her extra-sensory abilities.

When I went to see her for our weekly session, she said, *"Your light has expanded. You carry a lot of light within you and around you. There will be other beings, who people call the dark ones, who will come. They won't harm you, but they will appear to witness, and they can drain your light energy."*

She concluded our conversation by saying, *"Just keep your focus on the light."*

Well, I didn't understand much of what she said, and I sure as hell didn't want dark ones coming to me. I left her office a little unnerved and asked God to protect me from those beings.

I returned to work and shared what my mentor had said with my assistant.

Just as I uttered the words "*They will be coming,*" we felt an ominous sense in the air and heard a loud rumble outside. We looked out the window and saw a huge red truck pull into the driveway and park.

We heard the man get out of the car and then saw a little dog run up to the door, lift his leg, and pee on the door. At that moment, everything went into slow motion.

We felt doom walking, and we froze in place. I told my assistant not to be afraid and to stay very quiet. I then said to her, "*Please tell me you locked the door.*"

With a look of utter fear, she said, "*Oh God. No. I didn't. It's unlocked!*" I told her to pray as I whispered, "*God, please don't let him open the door, please don't let him open the door.*"

Then, the man appeared and peered through the door at us. God as my witness, there was no doubt this man was one of the dark ones my friend spoke of no more than an hour ago.

My assistant was pregnant, so I immediately stood in front of her to protect the baby from his energy. I didn't know that it would. *I just did it.*

We stood there and watched the man stretch out his hand to open the door to come in. However, when he touched the handle of the door, he immediately snatched it back as if his hand had been burned.

He tried to open the door three times, only to be met with the same result.

He could not open the door because *he was not being allowed to open the door.*

Right then, we realized we were divinely protected, and our faith became rock solid.

The experience ended with him peering through the door with a sinister grin. Then he pointed to me and mouthed, *I'll be back.*

A few days later, I was going to see a play with a friend. As we reached the curb to cross the street, I felt time slow down. I've experienced enough at this point to know that when time alters, something spiritual is about to happen.

I thought to myself, *"Okay. What now!"* I paused at the curb, sensing something was coming.

When I looked to my right, I saw an Old-timey Black *(1930s gangster style)* car approaching. As it passed in front of me unnaturally slow, I looked at the driver. He was a short man, dressed all in black, wearing a black top hat.

However, when I looked into his eyes, I knew who it was. He then smiled the same sinister grin as the man did at my salon the other day. It was the same man, only now sporting a different appearance.

Being fed up with his little tactics, I looked at him with pure disgust, flicked my wrist at him as if brushing him away, and said telepathically, *"Pfft! Dude, keep going. You can't touch me."*

After the play, a few hours later, my friend and I started to cross the street again, and darned if he didn't drive by again at the exact moment we hit the curb! This time I just shook my head, laughed, and kept walking.

I never saw either man, his truck, or the old-timey car again *until thirteen years later.*

I had a client come in, and she asked me to tell her of this experience again.

Even though I knew what we speak echoes everywhere and those we speak of would hear, I told her the story again.

Well, not to my surprise, the words were heard.

The very next day, I was driving down a country back road, and out of nowhere, there was the old-timey black car. I was driving too fast to see the driver, *but I didn't need to.* I knew it was the same spirit.

## No Vitals

For a few years after my near-death, out-of-body experience, when physicians would attempt to take my pulse or listen to my heartbeat, they couldn't find it.

They always ended up with a befuddled look on their face. At times, they even looked at me and said, *"I know you're alive. I can see you breathing."*

Even when I had the worst allergies, congestion, and asthma issues, they would listen to my lungs and say they were crystal clear. They often look puzzled because they know I have smoked for years.

When it came to my having blood taken, I often had to re-schedule because they couldn't find any blood to draw! After being stuck with the needle six or seven times, I being funny, began talking to the cells in my body, asking them to cooperate with the doctor. Surprisingly, we noticed my body would do as I asked!

We realized I could save myself a lot of unnecessary needle sticks, so now my body gets a talking-to *before* entering the doctor's office, and it works like a charm.

Though my initiation experiences sound wild, they taught me how to recognize perfect spirit guidance. They also provided me the spiritual power I would need for the coming years.

# Chapter Two

# The Signs

No matter how attached we become to physical matter,
our spirit will always return to the afterlife materially empty-handed.

## Bells

I was remarkably close to my Grandmother as she raised me most of my youth. We went through some of my most challenging teenage life experiences together.

As a young mother, I had spiritual beliefs, but practicing them was not my lifestyle.

The week my Gramma crossed over, I began hearing a dainty bell ringing through the air in my living room. Yet, I had *not one bell in my house*.

I knew without a doubt it was Gramma letting me know she was there.

I paid attention and recognized the bell would ring every evening around 8 p.m. There was no doubt in my mind that my Gramma appeared at 8 p.m. each night because that was the time I would put my son, her great-grandson, to bed. She absolutely adored him.

She was letting me know she was there to tuck him into bed and kiss him goodnight.

This continued for two weeks, and she then visited my aunt as my aunt said she had a similar experience.

My dad had also passed over around the same time as my Gramma. His message letting me know he was still present came in the morning time.

For a week after he crossed over, I would wake up each morning to see the picture frame that held his photo turned over.

## Candy Bars

My dear friend, Lupe, passed over unexpectedly. Everyone called her by her nickname, Loopy.

The day after Loopy crossed over, I stood in line at the grocery store, and my eyes went straight to a candy bar. To my amazement, I saw the candy bar had a new name cheekily called "Loopy."

I just smiled with a warm heart, knowing she was letting me know she was still hanging around, haha, And with a world-wide presence to boot!

She always did love her candy bars. Of course, I purchased it to honor her loving presence in my life.

That same day, I received a message from Loopy's sister. She said she, too, had been shopping and noticed the Loopy monikered candy bar.

Knowing how much Loopy loved candy bars, she said she knew it was Loopy sending her peace and comfort.

Neither of us had ever seen that candy bar on the shelf until the very day our dear Loopy crossed over.

## Children Know

After my friend Lupe crossed over, her sister emailed me, sharing an experience she encountered with Lupe's spirit.

She said she had been at her sister's funeral service, held at Lupe's home.

She was holding her granddaughter in her arms because the child was afraid and didn't want to be near anyone else.

*"Suddenly, my granddaughter looked at Lupe's room with curiosity and wanted to be put down,"* she recounted.

*"My granddaughter walked to Lupe's bedroom and just stood at the door staring at it as if she was staring into it. I knew right then, my sister was in her bedroom, and my sweet little girl knew it too."*

## Beyond Texting

My friend, who had a ten-month-old son, and I, were texting each other about how ignorant our human species can be at times.

I wrote, "*The children being born now will not be of that mentality. They, and your son, are here to teach the people with un-ascended minds how to be.*"

To my shocking surprise and gut-busting enjoyment, the text I received back was written in the Chinese language. Translated, it said, *"I not teach the poopies."*

My friend texted me back saying that her son had her phone in his hand, and when she went to respond, she saw what he had texted.

We laughed in utter amazement at his powerful message. Her son's soul-self bluntly revealed his purpose and his thoughts about un-ascended minds just as a child does, comically!

## He Peeps In

My father passed over many years ago. However, when my brother visited me, he learned that dad being invisible doesn't mean he's gone.

One of my brothers came up to visit for a few days.

I was walking through my bedroom with my cell phone in my hand. The phone decided to take a picture of my bedroom wall - all by itself, which happens quite often in my world.

I'm used to this kind of spiritual activity, so I knew it was spirit related.

When I looked at the image, I just laughed and thought, *How appropriate!*

I immediately showed it to my brother and asked, *"Who does that face on the wall look like to you?"*

His eyes got as wide as saucers, and he even looked a little afraid as he shouted, *"That's Dad! What the hell! How does that happen?"*

I just laughed and said, *"Welcome to my world. Dad was just popping in to say hi, letting you know he's still around."*

The deeper synchronicity between my dad and brother is that they share the same name and birthday.

## A Pearl of Wisdom

The day before my friend Lupe passed over, she left a message on my phone asking me to send her healing energy because she knew something was wrong with her.

I didn't receive the message until the next morning. That evening after work was when I planned to call her back, but before I could, Lupe's husband called to tell me she had passed away in the early hours of the day.

When looking through my journals to compile this book, I saw that Lupe had sent me three "sign-filled" text messages before she crossed over.

Lupe held a very symbolic consciousness, so when I received these messages, I knew they were important enough to save, but I didn't know how they connected - until now.

On my birthday, she sent, *"If you have an 'M' pattern on your palm, you're extremely gifted,"* which is something she always tried to get me to understand about myself.

The second message was on Christmas Day. It was a Nostradamus prediction referring to a blind mystic dying. She always referred to herself as a blind mystic.

The third message was on New Year's Day. It was her astrological reading that spoke of death and rebirth which, ended up taking place one month later.

Solemnly, I thought, had I paid attention to all these signs, maybe I could have helped her somehow.

However, I learned that was the point of my not speaking with her the night before she died.

In meditation, Lupe helped me understand a pearl of divine wisdom when it comes to life and death.

She transmitted, *"If you had known I was going to pass over, you would have interfered with my destiny and legacy - and yours."*


She awakened me to understand that how and when we die is already recorded within us, and trying to stop or prolong death only creates chaos at a soul level.

## You Are My Sunshine

After my mother's passing, my sister-in-law was making a memorial video for her and asked me what song I wanted to play on the video. With zero thought and out-of-the-blue, I replied, *"You Are My Sunshine."*

Choosing this song surprised me because I couldn't recall any connection between it and Mom. After organizing this book, however, I noticed throughout my journals I had mentioned this song to three different people - and *in every instance,* it referenced death and the afterlife.

My brother said not to make the song too sad, so I told my sister-in-law that maybe we should choose another song.

However, the deeper magic of the "Sunshine" song unfolded later that evening when I was video-chatting with my ten-year-old niece.

*"Aunt Jen, can I play two songs for you?"* she asked excitedly.

I said, *"Absolutely!"* I then said, *"OMG, it would be so amazing if you would play a special song for Nana at her memorial celebration! Nana would love that."*

She asked me which song she should play for Nana. I told her to make one up in her own special way that comes from her heart.

She then said, *"Oh, okay. I got it! Let me play two more songs for you, and the last one is the one I will play for Nana.*

*It's called... You Are My Sunshine!"*

I nearly fell out of my chair with awe. I told her that was the exact song I chose for Nana's video!

With our mouths open, we just stared at each other in awe of the magical synchronicity. Then she played Nana's song perfectly.

This mystical moment was also the perfect opportunity for me to talk with my niece about her Nana still being alive and always with us. So we delved into a deep discussion about the spirit world.

Then, we both heard a mysterious swishing sound move through the air in her room.

She looked around the room curiously and said, very naturally and factually, *"Oh, that's Nana."*

Comforted that she knew and understood our loved ones are still alive and with us, I agreed. We ended our video chat with my being a very proud Auntie Jen!

Later that evening, my Mom showed me a vision of herself kissing her granddaughter and grandson (my niece and nephew) on the forehead when they were in bed asleep.

Her point clearly reveals, *"Our loved ones are always present, and we don't need a physical body to continue the love."*

## Gettin' 'Er Done

My friend Lupe and I spent a lot of time remote-viewing and enhancing our extra-sensory abilities together. Remote-viewing is the ability to see into other locations or dimensions with the mind's eye.

As a reflection of her soul's identity, I always called her *"My Little Catholic Nun,"* and as a reflection of mine, she always called me *"Scary Fairy."*

She always said I could scare the awakening into anyone. Ha-ha. Lupe was my greatest advocate when it came to my spiritual work.

Even though people and religions persecute those with meta-physical abilities, Lupe always wanted to publicize my spiritual work. She genuinely wanted people to learn about their soul-self and the glorious connections they were missing in life.

She pushed me for years to go public, and every time she did, I would shut her down. I had already dipped my toes in the spotlight once, which catalyzed my demand for privacy thereafter, and I had every intention of keeping it that way.

Her favorite comeback was, *"You know, Scary Fairy, if God wants it done, it will get done."* - *"So true,"* I'd laugh and say.

Not too long after Lupe's passing, I had a client whose loved one had recently crossed over, and she was having a hard time with the loss.

One morning, I received a vision and message from her loved one, so I texted the information to her.

When I picked up my phone to text a follow-up message to my grieving client, I noticed the previous text message had *NOT* been sent to her.

I discovered I had instead accidentally sent it to a *very religious* friend who is totally closed to the idea of mystical abilities. To make matters worse, she was also well known as the town gossip.

*Um, Panic!*

As if that snafu wasn't "public" enough, in a few agonizing seconds more, I recognized the text I sent actually went out as a group message to *everyone* in my friend's rigidly religious group!

I immediately knew it was all Loopy's doing and shouted out loud, *"Loopy!!!"*

I eventually laughed the situation off and said, "*Well, Loopy, you finally got what you wanted! The whole dang town will know my stuff now!*"

Then I heard Lupe's sneaky little giggle in the distance as she spouted her familiar phrase, *"Gettin' 'er done."*

The only text I received back from my friend was, *"Who is this?"*

When I responded with an apology for texting the wrong people, no one responded, and the thread stopped.

My so-called friend never said a word about the text. Shortly after the incident, however, she stopped communicating with me, which was not a surprise.

I guarantee you my sweet Lupe is dancing in the heavens over my writing this book!

## Sister Love

Not long after my friend Lupe passed over, her sister shared a beautiful experience and her moment of awakening.

*"I get pretty bad migraines,"* she began.

*"I got up around three a.m. overnight and walked to the kitchen. I saw a spirit appear, and I knew it was Lupe. She was a little taller and thinner now - which is what she always wanted to be. Ha-ha."*

*"I was so angry when she passed,"* she continued.

*"I thought, why her? Lupe always said I feared the spirit world, and that's why I don't feel it and understand it."*

She ended her message and her heartache, saying, "Now, seeing Lupe in spirit this way, I'm not angry or afraid anymore because I still sense her presence, and I smell her perfume often."

## Get Him Out of My Bed

A very dear friend of mine was in the hospital with severe heart issues. She had been in an induced coma.

When she came to, I noticed she had a different look in her eyes. They were dark and somewhat empty, indicating that her spirit-soul had recently visited the afterlife.

With a bit of anger and a bizarre look on her face, she asked me, *"Who's that man sitting on the bed next to me?"*

Even though I knew it was likely a spirit guide to lead her to the afterlife, I said, *"I don't know,"* I replied. *"Maybe it's a spirit guide here to help you get well."*

She had a deep, dark look in her eyes, and in a voice not of her own, said angrily, *"I don't want him here. Get him out of my bed."*

*"Okay,"* I said. *"I will ask him to leave."*

Both verbally and telepathically, I asked the spirit to leave.

After a minute or so, I asked my friend if he was gone. She looked over to where he sat and, with a strange skepticism, said, *"Yes. I don't want him back here again."*

My friend crossed over a few days later.


I had an intuitive sense that once my friend crossed over, she made friends with that helping spirit after all!

## Spirit Maintenance

My friend and I owned and operated a restaurant together. One day when at work, we noticed a light bulb was out in one of our lamps.

We didn't have any extra bulbs on hand, but the cafe was closed, so it wasn't a big deal. We figured we would put a bulb in the next day.

However, I felt led to call on spirit and ask for the spirit guide that tends to maintenance repairs to fix the light for us.

I wasn't sure the spirit world had handyman spirits, but I figured *you never know.*

Then my friend and I went into the kitchen and began prepping.

The next time we went into the dining area, the light was on!

My friend and I just laughed in our moment of awe and yelled out, *"Thank you, handyman spirit!"*

We were the only *people* in the cafe that day. I guess there really are maintenance spirits!

## Hotel Girl

I was working part-time at a hotel that had a history of spirit activity.

One day, a family of guests came to the front desk very unnerved.

They explained to the manager they could not get any sleep because of strange things happening in the room.

They said they were up all night listening to a child crying mysteriously.

They soon realized the place was haunted by a spirit when the phone in their room started moving across the table all by itself.

Trying to reason away their inexplicable experience, all they kept repeating was, *"But, we're Christians. We don't believe in this stuff."*

Trying with all my might not to bust out with laughter, I thought to myself, *"They're believers now!"*

## Destined Love

My sister-in-law once shared an incredible story of destined love with me.

She said her mother told her that when she was pregnant with her, her parents thought they would have a boy and had planned on naming the boy Russell.

But, later, they found out they were having a girl instead.

Curiously, when my future sister-in-law was in fourth grade, she said she had signed her name on her Cabbage Patch Doll adoption card.

However, she wrote her last name as "Russell." Yet, Russell was not her last name.

Then, surprise, surprise, as a teen, she met the man she was destined to marry, my brother *Russell*.

She married him at the age of twenty-one, and they have been each other's breath ever since.

Ironically, she and I also share the exact same first, middle, and last names.

Sounds to me like destiny is in charge, and not humans!

## Soul to Soul

I share this experience to reveal the depths of spiritual love and the lifelong impact we have on people and their lives.

I met Dub, one of my soulmates, when I was in sixth grade. Being too young to know any more than kid's stuff, we knew we were mysteriously connected within but didn't know why and why we couldn't stay together.

This wasn't a big deal with us because we ended up dating off and on through the years.

One day, the sidewalk we walked every day to school was being paved. I adored Dub so much that I took a stick and wrote *"Dub and Jen Forever"* in the wet cement.

He always said that throughout his life, every time he walked down that sidewalk, he would stop to read it and feel the love, remembering us.

When we were eighteen, he decided to give me a ring to symbolize our unity, honoring our possible future together. This was a big deal for him because he had never made such a statement to anyone else.

I, however, at that time had no idea just how important it was to him.

Dub was a musician. His days consisted of hanging with the guys in the band, playing music, and smoking weed. I, however, was working in a demanding job in the corporate world.

When I had time off, I had no desire to hang with the gang listening to music. I wanted to be with him and to do enjoyable activities together.

After asking if he would go to a birthday event with me, he responded by saying he had to rehearse with the guys. I'd had enough.

As he was rehearsing at his friend's house, I put the ring on his dresser with a note saying that our relationship was over - *and why.*

The only response I received was a song dedication to me. He called into a radio station and had them play a heart-wrenching song, "Behind Blue Eyes," for my birthday. This opposed the love song he wrote for me, "Behind Green Eyes." But we did not end there. *We never ended.*

Throughout the years, we would always mysteriously reappear in each other's lives when we were experiencing significant life events. We were always there for each other briefly and then separate again.

Thirteen years passed before we reconnected again. Again, we rejoined when a major life event was happening.

One day, a mutual friend of ours called me, saying, *"You need to call Dub. He needs to hear your voice."*

When I asked him why - my heart leaped from my chest as he told me that my dear soulmate had been diagnosed with brain cancer.

I immediately hung up and called him. When he answered the phone, I melted inside, like I always did, when I heard his loving voice.

He said, "Hi, sweety. I hadn't moved from the chair all day until I saw your number show on the phone. I said, Ah, that's my Jen, and I ran to answer it."

Then what came out of his mouth took my breath and life away.

He said, *"Jen, will you answer a question I've had?"* Agreeing, he asked, *Why did you break up with me and give my ring back?*

Weak in the knees, I fell backward onto the couch to sit. My heart ached, knowing he had held this inside for over twenty years.

I reminded him of the scene and that I had told him the reason that day long ago. He said, with sadness, *"Yeah, All the girls I've dated said the same thing."*

I knew the soul love we had between us was so deep that it would help him somehow. I had hoped hearing the answer to his lifelong question helped free him in some way.

We continued a lovely conversation. Then I experienced my own life-altering awakening after we hung up. I realized the *long-lasting* impact our actions can have on other lives. We can never know what our judgments and decisions actually do to another person and their life path.

Now Dub and I had a deep love for each other, and we dated many times after returning the ring, but that wasn't what he held deep in his heart.

Just as we had begun, stayed, and concluded, another major event reconnected us, and I knew it was to keep our love intact - for his crossover.

Before my sweet Dub entered the life beyond us, I recalled a beautiful, *divinely orchestrated* fact. Since the last time Dub and I had been together, which was thirteen years, I had not been involved with anyone else.

When I told Dub he was the last man I had kissed, we were filled with a deep inner peace - and knowing that we would be together again one day.

Just as we began, two children joined for a lifelong journey together, he left this world, sending me a love note inside a hand-drawn heart... "D.W. and J.B. Forever."

*And our "forever" continued.*

He, in spirit, appeared a few days after his crossing. He transmitted his love, spiritual guidance, and a new song for me to remember... *"Benny and the Jets."*

Visible or not, no one's journey ever ends.

## A Bright Light Shines

I had met two new friends, Han and Jan. I knew their daughter had passed away at a young age and that it was a sensitive subject, so I never asked about the details.

On my way to visit them one day, it was unusually dark and foggy. The fog was so thick I could barely see to drive.

As I was nearing their home, I felt a sudden strangeness fill the air and knew a spirit was present.

Out of the blue, the ominous sky parted in front of me, and a tremendously bright light beamed down, mysteriously shining only on my car.

This light shined down for a few minutes before disappearing as quickly as it came. I knew this was a sign of their daughter's presence.

When I arrived, I wasn't sure how to bring up the subject. Then, it just came out. I shared my experience with Han, letting him know the light that came to me was his daughter. Han then lowered his head with a sense of sadness.

I apologized for bringing up such a sensitive subject and told him the experience with her was so beautiful, I felt he should know she was still with them and always accessible.

I continued to tell him of another interconnected mystery I often experience when driving to their house, which also took place in the same location.

I explained, *"Every time I get to this one area of the road, where the light appeared, my music cd mysteriously switches to play a certain song. The song is a lullaby."*

I continued explaining to him this happens every time I reach that one area, and I felt the lullaby references a childhood memory between them.

Then a heartwarming smile replaced Han's moment of sadness. He looked up at me and told me about the day his daughter died.

"*She had an accident trying to save her dog,*" he said. "*That day was a dark, gloomy day, just like today.*"

He continued, saying, "*I sat on a rock praying as I watched the paramedics try to revive her.*

*Then, an incredible light beam came from the heavens and shone down, and only on her body - nowhere else. When I saw the light shining only on her, I knew she wasn't staying.*"

He then told me she had died in the area where I saw her light beam down on me that day - and that he knew what the lullaby meant.

# Chapter Three

# The Mysteries

The divine never separate themselves from us.
It is humankind who separates themselves from the
divine.

## Spirit Bubbles

One of the most majestic encounters I've experienced happened when the dogs and I were walking at a lake.

I was in a walking meditation and called upon the spirits of nature to come forth and walk with us. The wind suddenly increased and blew a warm, gentle breeze over me.

I felt as if the most beautiful spirit was filling the sky. I stopped and briefly meditated on the sunlight reflecting upon the water.

As I began walking again, I looked up to the sky and saw a strange, deep-yellow haze descending. I assumed it was a dust cloud from a passing car. However, as it drifted closer to me, the cloud was actually a group of misty golden circles.

As they floated toward me, they began to expand outward.

Thinking my vision was impaired, I rubbed my eyes and blinked a few times only to find the circles were still there, gently hovering above and in front of me.

Mystified, I walked closer to them and counted about fifty circles in various sizes. The larger circles changed their color to a deep gold as they descended closer to me.

I noticed my dog, Dakota, sitting quietly beside me. He was mesmerized, too, as the circles came upon us. I felt like a little kid, giggling as the golden circles floated through us.

After a few moments, the circles began to slowly retreat and ascend. They hovered in the sky for a moment as if saying goodbye, and I thanked them for their blessing as I watched them slowly disappear into the atmosphere.

## True Prayer

I had developed a cyst on my neck due to the seatbelt impact during my car accident.

I was scheduled to have the cyst surgically removed, and quite nervous about the procedure because it was located between my jugular and carotid arteries.

The day before my surgery, a man who happened to be a minister came into my salon for a haircut. We spoke about the surgery, and before he left, he said, *"I would like to pray with you for your surgery tomorrow."*

I was touched and responded, *"Absolutely. I am very grateful for your blessing."*

He held my hands in his and began his prayer. *"Lord, I pray that you take care of my sister. Bring to her steady hands, easy healing, and your divine miracle,"* he said. *"I pray now for the cyst to pop right out of her neck."*

I thought his description was such an odd way of putting it; however, I was thankful for his presence and prayer, so I gave it no more thought.

The next day, I went into surgery. I had forgotten all about the man who prayed for me until the doctor came in after the operation.

The surgeon entered my room with a quirky smile and said the surgery was a cakewalk.

Then he shook his head with a smile and slight disbelief and said, *"I've never seen anything like it before. When I made the incision, the cyst just popped right of your neck."*

I immediately remembered the man's descriptive prayer and told the doctor about the man who prayed for me. He smiled as if he knew and said he had a lot of patients tell him of similar situations.

He then handed me a mirror and said, *"Now, don't freak out. Your neck looks like the Bride of Frankenstein right now, but it won't stay that way."*

I laughed and said, *"Honey, you didn't cut my jugular or carotid, I'm breathing, and I had a stranger's prayer come true. I'm good with the Bride of Frankenstein thing!"*

I never saw the man who prayed for me again. I have no doubt he was led to my salon with powerful energy to help me in my time of need.

# Watching George

I had spent eighteen years in business with Shaw, the owner of the property where I once rented my salon space.

I often told him and his wife that I spent more of my life with them than anyone else, even my own family. After almost two decades, Shaw decided to sell the property, and I had to move my salon.

When I moved into my new location, I took a few pictures of the exterior to put on my website. As I looked through the images, I noticed a male spirit standing inside the new salon, looking out the window at me.

One day, the property manager and I were outside talking, and I told her about the spirit presence in my window. When I showed her the picture, her eyes widened, and her mouth dropped open.

She jumped up and said, *"Come with me!"* She took me into her office and pointed to a portrait of a man on the wall.

I said, *"That's him! That's the man who was standing inside my salon!"*

*"I know,"* she said. *"That is George, the man who owns this property. He died the weekend before you moved in."*

As if the George sighting weren't enough, when I told Shaw where my new salon was, he laughed at the synchronicity, saying, *"I used to own that building too."*

Then we both laughed at the mystery when he reminded me that he had also built the condominium where I lived.

*Me thinks destiny is some pretty deep stuff!*

## I'm Here!

One afternoon, I was in the kitchen at my friend's house, prepping for us to have dinner together.

All of a sudden, we heard a loud bang come from the living room. Something had hit the wall forcefully.

Puzzled, I walked out to see what it could be. I noticed the angel sun-catcher, which had been in my friend's bedroom, was now lying on the living room floor.

Evidently, a spirit had removed the sun-catcher from her bedroom window, taken it to the living room, and hurled it at the wall.

I asked my friend which spirits she had been talking to recently, and she said she had been talking with her Mom every night before bed.

My friend said she knew when the spirits of her Mom and husband were around because she could feel them. She said they always helped her figure things out or find something she had lost.

I said, *"Well, I guess your Mom making a ruckus means she's joining us for dinner!"*

## Sky Beings

**W**hen it comes to taking photos, I typically only take pictures when I am spiritually led. When I do, I often capture strange, mystical images.

To this day, I have no idea what the native triangle pattern shown below was hovering in the sky.

On another occasion, while driving to work, I felt led to pull over and take pictures of a specific tree.

When I looked at the images, I was a little taken back. I had captured a few images revealing various reptilian patterns spanning the sky surrounding the sun.

Another image revealed only what I could refer to as a metallic being wearing a reptilian-patterned chest shield.

There were also two round objects with lights hovering in the sky behind it.

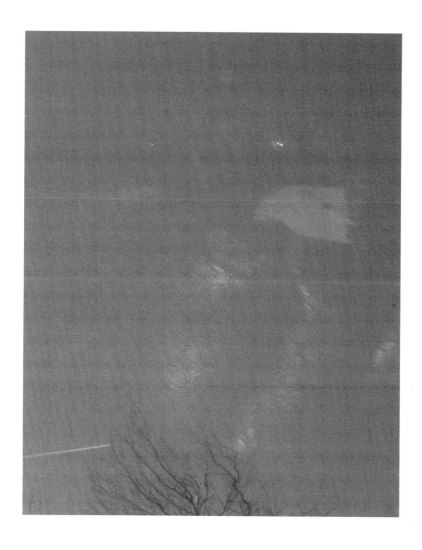

## Tower Man

At one point in time, I worked the evening shift at a spiritually active hotel with a presence we called "The Tower Man."

This presence was the spirit of an old maintenance man who had tended to the hotel for many years. When I connected with him spiritually, I felt he wasn't a very friendly fellow, but he never bothered anyone.

One evening three women checked into the hotel. I gave them their key, and they went to their shared room, which happened to be next to the Tower Man's room. About an hour later, they came to the desk and asked me if the hotel was haunted. I laughed and asked, *"Why? What did you feel?"*

They shared that when they passed by a particular room, his room, they felt a creepy energy, and they knew there was a spirit presence in there.

They also asked if their room was connected to another guest's room. I said, *"No. In fact, you are the only guests here tonight. Why?"*

They looked at each other a little unnerved and said, *"We heard a man's voice talking through the vent in our room."*

I smiled and told them that other people have reported experiencing the same thing and I, too, often heard voices coming from the vent at my desk. I reassured them the Tower Man didn't bother anyone and asked if they wanted me to move them to a new room.

They chuckled and said, *"Um, yes, please - far away from his."*

## Creatures and Bugs

I went to work one day, and as I always do, I went through each room, turning on lights and cleaning up.

My therapy room had always been spiritually active, so I never knew what I would find when I opened the door.

On this particular day, when I entered my therapy room, I walked past a chair and noticed an odd imprint on the seat. When I looked closer, the heebie-jeebies got all over me!

The pattern on the chair was clearly an imprint of an other-worldly bug - *a very large bug.*

As I investigated its substance, it appeared to be some sort of gray dust.

However, when I tried to remove it with my hand and then a rag, it wouldn't come off. I then realized it was made of a greasy, ashy substance.

With cleaner and some scrubbing, I finally removed the substance from the chair, but not before taking a picture for proof. I knew I needed evidence because my friends would surely think I was wack-a-doodled when they heard my story.

A similar situation later occurred with that same chair. One day, when I walked into the therapy room, I saw that the chair had two large creature-like handprints imprinted on the back of it.

The fingerprints were long and claw-like, and they stretched over the chair's back as if a creature had crawled over the top of it. When I tried to clean the handprints from the chair, they consisted of the same greasy, ashy substance as the otherworldly bug.

Years later, when I entered my salon one morning, I found the same long-fingered claw marks on the floor in the styling area where a therapy tray filled with sand sat on the table.

Mysteriously, *something* had taken sand from the tray overnight and thrown it on the floor. I say thrown because the tray had not been moved. It was still in its regular place on the table, showing no sign of being disturbed.

I noticed the sand on the floor had the same long-fingered claw markings as the therapy chair once had. The only difference was that this imprint did not have the waxy ash substance.

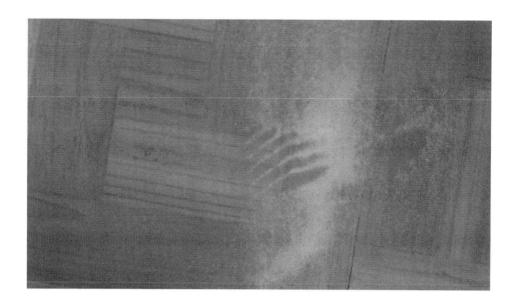

I guess this spirit got bored overnight and decided to do a little sand-art!

## Prayed Up!

I went to a friend's house to do an ear candling on her Mom, who had been deaf in one ear for years. Ear candling is an ancient process of cleansing the inner ears.

When I finished the treatment, my friend's Mom sat up in bed with a shocked look on her face and exclaimed, *"Praise Jesus! I can hear out of my deaf ear!"*

Instantly, I tapped her on the forehead and said, *"Praise Jesus! You've been healed!"*

After a few moments of laughter, she asked, *"How did that happen? How can I hear out of that ear now?"*

My friend giggled, pointing to me, and said, *"That's Jen's Hoodjie-Woodjie!"* I chuckled and just pointed to the heavens.

Her Mom then said, with an absolute look of knowing on her face and in a voice that didn't sound like her own, *"You've been praying, haven't you? You got yourself all prayed up."*

I had recently been praying a lot and was not surprised it was being acknowledged. I just laughed and said, *"Amazing things happen when you're all prayed up!"*

## Shadow Man

One day while my friend and I were working at the cafe, not to my surprise, spirit presence was again the focus.

As we chopped veggies in the kitchen, I happened to look up and see an enormous "shadow being" fly very quickly in front of us. He was wearing a long black cloak and a black hat.

I see spirit activity all the time, so it didn't faze me. I didn't mention it to my friend because she had always said it creeps her out when she sees spirits. So as not to alarm her, I just kept chopping the veggies.

To my surprise, however, she looked over at me with wide eyes and said, *"Did you see that?!"*

I laughed and said, *"OMG, you saw that?"*

She said, *"Yes! What the hell was that?"*

I simply responded saying, *"Exactly what you think, a shadow spirit."*

When I explained that shadow spirits are those who have died in a quick, traumatic way and they don't actually see us or our surroundings, our hearts were filled with compassion.

We sent him heartfelt love, and I prayed for the being's spiritual freedom that evening.

Thank you, Shadow Man, for proving to my friend that I am really not crazy - *or that she's as crazy as I am!*

## Little Timmy

One of the most heartwarming spiritual moments I've experienced was when I worked at a hotel, where a coworker once shared a story about a six-year-old boy named Timmy.

Back in the 1960s, Timmy's dad was building the hotel next door. One day Timmy accompanied his father to the construction site. Tragically, Timmy fell from the rafters and died.

My heart was heavy with compassion for Timmy and his dad. I couldn't imagine what they went through. I told my coworker that I would love to meet Timmy's spirit if just to let him know he is loved and remembered. Even after our conversation ended, I just could not stop thinking about him.

Later that evening, a wicked snowstorm blew in. I stood at a bay window in our hotel, staring out at the storm. Suddenly, it felt like time just stopped. I thought to myself, that must be one hell of a storm to be able to alter time.

Then, out of nowhere, I see a child appear under the portico. He looked at me, smiled, and waved to me just as a happy child does.

At this point, everything appeared to be taking place in slow motion, but my thoughts were at hyper speed. I had a concerned, confused look on my face as I smiled and waved back to him.

I worried about him being out in such a bad storm alone, and I wondered where his parents were. I noticed he wasn't wearing the proper clothing to survive being out in that kind of weather. He only had on a puffy vest and sweatpants.

As I looked a little closer, I noticed something looked different about him. He just stood there looking at me as if giving my mind time to catch on.

I decided I needed to get him and bring him inside. As I started toward the door, I saw a group of guests pass by him. I thought perhaps they were his parents, but they walked right in front of him, and no one acknowledged him.

On my way out to get him, I met the guests and asked if the child was theirs.

They looked at me as if I were crazy and said, *"What child? We didn't see any child out there."*

I left them quite confused and went to look around outside, but the child had disappeared. As I stood there in dead silence, the wind picked up, and I heard the name "Timmy" echo through me.

Right then, I knew the little boy was Timmy in spirit, and I knew he felt my heart call to him.

I called my coworker and told him of the experience, explaining what the child looked like and what he was wearing. My coworker said, *"You just described Timmy. He died in the fall season."*

I was so touched that little Timmy trusted me enough to share himself with me, and I was also glad to know he was present and happy.


While I frequently felt his presence, Timmy never visually appeared to me again.

## Roping Creature

About a week before Archangel Michael informed me that I would be entering "two years of darkness," I had a visit from an unusual creature who appeared on my deck.

One day, I was led to go look out my sliding glass window. As I did, I saw a short, chubby creature standing there gazing out at the mountain sky.

I knew this creature was a "reaper" who comes to prepare the path for endings and transitions. I, of course, became a little concerned, wondering what kind of ending was in store for me.

The creature must have known I was watching because it turned around and looked directly at me. I noticed it was holding a natural corded rope in its hand.

I watched as it began running back and forth, making a looping action around my deck. The creature made three looping passes in an oval pattern around my entire deck.

I sensed it might have been making some sort of invisible barrier of protection. Of course, I wondered, protection from what?

When the creature completed its job, it looked over at me, jumped up into the air, and disappeared. I didn't worry too much about the experience because, honestly, I felt the little dude was somehow helping me.

When the "clicking beings" appeared soon after, I knew exactly what the little creature's actions were about.

Like all spirits, the reaper knew exactly what would happen, and it prepared the way.

## Clicking Beings

After getting comfy in bed one night, I began to hear a strange, out-of-this-world sound coming from my deck.

I was lying on my side, my back to the deck. The noise sounded so creepy I just laid still. I adopted the *"what I don't know won't bother me"* intelligence and had no intention of rolling over to see what it was.

My dogs also heard the noise. Both sat up, on guard, looking out the window. I next heard what I could only describe as a spaceship sound in the air. Whatever it was landed on my deck.

I hadn't ever given much focus to alien beings, so I figured it had to be the wind simply sounding like a spaceship...until my dogs jumped off the bed in full-on attack mode, barking at the window.

I didn't know if the beings could see us or try to come in, so I was quite freaked out. I stressfully whispered to the dogs to be quiet and get back on the bed. I did not want *whatever they were* to know we were inside.

The dogs returned to the bed, and I grabbed hold of them. I kept praying, *"God, please don't let them see us. Please don't let them see us."*

Then, a high-pitched sound hit the air, making everything silent, and I heard what sounded like a pressurized door open.

As if that weren't enough to scare me out of my skin, I then heard two beings walking on my deck. One went to one end of the deck and the other to the other end.

As I lay there, frozen in place, my dogs strangely didn't move a muscle either.

I listened as the two beings began to communicate with each other in a "clicking" language. One would click in a sequence of clicks, then the other would respond similarly.

As I listened, I noticed the dogs were listening too. They cocked their heads as each being clicked. The beings spoke (clicked) back and forth for a few minutes.

While they communicated with each other, I sensed they were unaware the dogs and I were inside.

While this was a rare experience, nearly equal parts chilling and thrilling in retrospect, at the time, I just wanted the beings to go.

I thankfully soon heard the "craft" start, the pressurized door close, and the visitors left.

Having no desire to sleep, It dawned on me that the reason the beings didn't seem to be aware the dogs and I were inside was due to what the roping creature had done on my deck.

Then again, that little reaper may have been making some type of landing strip! Either way, I felt what the deck creature had done with the rope cloaked us from the clicking beings.

Why they chose my balcony out of all the other houses in the world was beyond me. Being deeply curious, I decided to call the not-for-profit Mutual UFO Network (MUFON) to report the incident.

The lead investigator called me back and informed me there had been increased reports in my area.

He explained what I had described had been reported by many people before.

When I asked him why the visitors chose my deck, he laughed and said, *"You must be a psychic or an energy-sensitive person because they often connect with people who have extra-sensory abilities. Next time it happens,"* he continued, *"be sure to look and take pictures."*

"I replied, *"Yeh, that's SO not gonna happen!"*

I didn't worry about these otherworldly beings appearing again because, honestly, I felt completely protected. I had no further contact with these clicking beings - *until seven years later.*

## We're Baaaack

A new client came to my salon for hair services. She was visiting the area on vacation, and we connected instantly. She asked me to join her for dinner and conversation at her place one evening.

I arrived at her short-term rental as planned, and we enjoyed an evening of higher-consciousness conversation. During our discussion, she asked me if I believed in alien life forms and otherworldly beings.

I responded with a chuckle, saying, *"Well, I wasn't sure at first, but then I had an experience that made me wonder."* I continued by telling her about the "clicking beings."

She smiled and shared, *"Well, let me tell you something. Every night I've been here, I have heard a clicking sound coming from the closet.*

*I have searched the closet and the entire apartment for an explanation and found no source for the clicking."*

I shook my head mindlessly as I remembered my experience and said, "Well, now I'm really going to blow your mind. When I experienced the clicking beings on my deck, I lived in the apartment right above this one."

She asked me how to stop them from communicating. I said the only thing I could think of: *"Just open the closet door and tell them you are not interested in communicating."*

I told her being direct typically works in the spirit world, and maybe it would work here, too.

She called me the next day and said she did just that, and the clicking promptly stopped.

## Money Game

For some *ding-dong* reason, I decided to hide a portion of my money in a canister at a place I worked.

Well, that ended up not being such a brilliant idea because when I went to retrieve it, the canister was gone.

I then recalled throwing three canisters in the trash when I had been cleaning the week before.

I continued to look everywhere, but I drew the line at dumpster diving. So I let it go and resolved that someone obviously needed the money more than I did.

At home later that evening, I decided to clean out my bathroom cabinet. When I opened the cabinet door, I spotted a canister like the one I had put my money in.

I thought there was no way it could be the missing canister because I absolutely knew I did not bring it home. Even if I had, I would have never put it under the bathroom sink, for goodness' sake!

Nonetheless, when I opened the lid, there was my money inside. All I could do was shake my head and laugh!

I gave thanks and concluded the spirits were either playing a money game or just letting me know they "have my back."

## Damn, That's Good

My very proper and politically correct beau and I had decided to go to church one Sunday.

As the entire congregation stood listening to the choir sing that morning, I stood next to him with my eyes closed, totally connected with the choir's heavenly sound.

Suddenly, I heard a high-pitched sound piercing my eardrums, and I went completely deaf to the church choir. I was left hearing a single majestic voice singing from the far distance, sounding like the most melodic angel in heaven.

I cannot begin to describe what the tone sounded like specifically or what it did to me, but it was the most ethereal sound I had ever heard in my life.

As the angel blanketed me with her lullaby, I knew I had heard her voice somewhere before as I became one with her.

Entranced, I no longer perceived I was in church or that other people were even present. I didn't know how long I was unified with this angelic voice, but at some point, I felt a tugging on my dress.

I opened my groggy eyes and looked over at my beau. He had a look of pure shock on his face.

I then looked around the church and noticed everyone else was already sitting down. They were all looking at me, including the priest, who appeared to be waiting for me so he could continue.

Filled with embarrassment, my beau yanked on my dress again and said, *"Sit down. Oh, my God, sit down."*

With that, I fell backward into our pew, and on my way down, my head grazed the head of the man sitting directly behind me.

Still dazed and confused from the angelic voice, I looked at my beau with a joyful smile and said (quite loudly, I might add), *"Damn, that was good! Now that's the way church should be!"*

*I can't even tell you how mortified he was.*

When church was over, he couldn't get out of there fast enough. He walked to the car as fast as he could and left me in the dust!

When I got in the car, I was still a little groggy. He recapped the whole event and said, *"Jen, you were the only one standing after everyone else sat down! And to make it worse, while you were standing there, you swayed back and forth with a goofy smile on your face - while everyone watched you!"*

I laughed so hard I thought I would fall out of the car.

He then said, *"Oh my God, I was so embarrassed. I'm never going to church with you again."*

Still laughing, I simply said, *"Dude, you missed out! It was amazing! That's how everyone should be in church!"*

*It was an incredibly quiet ride home.*

## Witches and Invisible Cars

After my "standing-room-only" church experience revealing what church *should be*, I experienced what church should *NOT* be.

One night, I had a dream vision revealing how God and the divine guides communicate with us through our dreams and daily experiences.

Afterward, I was spiritually led to deliver that message to the priest of the church I was attending as a subject he might consider discussing in services.

I thought how lovely it would be for people to be able to see God in every experience instead of just one day a week.

As led, I wrote out the vision message and was guided to drop it in the church's suggestion box. However, I chickened out and decided not to do it.

I knew if I shared that message, I would be persecuted as being *witchy* or possessed by evil.

By this time in my life, I was so sick of hearing people condemning others. I wanted no part of that ignorance anymore. However, always open to divine guidance, I tucked the note in my purse anyway and went to church.

I concluded the note would stay in my purse, and I would not deliver it. Yet, as I walked through the church doors, slow motion kicked in, and I knew what that meant - *no Jennifer choices today.*

With wide eyes and a gasping breath, I watched my hand extend outward ever so gracefully toward the suggestion box with the note in its grip.

My brain said, *"Oh, no! Are you kidding me?"*

Then I watched as the note gracefully fell into the suggestion box. I stood there looking at the box and thought about asking the priest to retrieve it for me.

However, without intention, I took a seat, knowing I should just suck it up and roll with it. The divine guides needed that message delivered - *and so it was.*

The following Sunday, I returned to the church. I had forgotten all about the note by that time. That is until I heard the priest's topic of discussion.

Surprise, surprise, surprise... the subject on tap was *witches, wizards, and false prophets!*

As he spoke, the priest often looked directly at me. I snickered with a sideways grin and just shook my head at him.

Right then, I knew I would not ever return to that church. Little did I know, I was about to learn another reason why I wouldn't return.

When the service was over, it was pouring down rain. I had no umbrella. As I walked to my car, I stopped dead in my tracks, shocked at what I saw. My car was gone. It was not where I had parked it. That spot was now empty.

I was in disbelief, walking around the parking lot confused and distraught. By this time, I was completely soaked; you could see through my clothes.

All the churchgoers were leaving, and every one of them drove right past me. I watched multiple cars drive by, and some people even looked right at me, sopping wet and clearly in distress. Not one person stopped to ask if I needed help.

I finally gave up the search. My car was nowhere in the lot. Resigned that someone had stolen my car and none of the church people were going to help me, I turned to go back inside the church to call a friend for a ride.

Suddenly, I mysteriously pivoted around and took one more look around the parking lot. Well, *lo and behold,* there was my car! It was parked in the exact spot I had left it!

With a huge sigh of relief, I headed for my car. When I got inside, I sat there soaking wet, thoroughly ticked off at the priest and the hypocrites. I laid my head on the steering wheel, exhausted from stress.

Then I began smiling with gratitude knowing I had just received the blessing of divine truth. I had been blessed to have witnessed *the real* witches, wizards, and false prophets.

More importantly, I knew for a fact that God is present in every experience I have - *just as my vision and note revealed.*

That was the last time I went to church. However, the revelation didn't end there.

When I told a friend about my car disappearing and reappearing, she looked at me as if I had lost my mind, judging my statement from every direction.

I simply said, *"Whatever. You will believe in spirit when this stuff happens to you!"*

Well, about week later, she called me on the phone, completely wigged out.

She said she had been shopping one day, and when she went back to her vehicle, it was gone.

*"My car was freaking invisible!"* she exclaimed. *"Then it reappeared a few minutes later, exactly where I parked it."*

*Believe me,* people on the other side of the planet could have heard me laughing!

## Lance and Cooper

To reveal that life here and beyond is an infinite union with the divine mystery, I share a profound journey my life-long friend Lillian experienced with her son.

One day, Lillian's nine-year-old son Lance asked his Mom if he could go outside and ride his bike. She said yes.

Lillian told me whenever Lance would go outside to play, he always said, *"See ya later, Mommy."*

This day, he turned to her and said, *"Goodbye, Mommy."*

His comment chilled her to the bone, and she knew it was a sign of trouble.

Lillian quickly grabbed him like a vice grip by his jacket collar to hold him back. She said, *"Sweety, why don't you stay inside and play with Mommy today?"*

Lillian explained that as she spoke those words, something strange and not of her doing happened.

*"I watched in slow motion as my hand mysteriously released from his collar,"* she recalled. *"I just stood there gripping thin air looking at my hand."*

She knew right then that she had no control over the situation, as Lance went outside to ride his bike.

Lillian was stunned and said she just sat on the couch waiting for the phone to ring. Just as she had known, the police shortly notified her that her son had been hit by a car.

Lance was taken to the hospital. He was okay, having no injuries other than a bit of fluid on the brain. The doctor expected medication would remedy the swelling. However, after a few days, the swelling had significantly increased.

Lillian held her son's hand one last time as she processed the news. Her son died that day.

A mother's worst nightmare was in play. However, time revealed the reason her son departed this world at such a young age.

See, Lillian was in an abusive relationship with her husband, Lance's father. It was clear that Lance left to break the bond of abuse, which ultimately saved his Mom.

Lillian left her abusive husband after Lance crossed over.

Later, Lillian had an intuitive friend confirm the same information. However, he went one step further, telling her that Lance would come back and be in her life again one day.

Many years later, Lillian decided to adopt two siblings from foster care, Bono and his younger brother Cooper. I was so happy she had children in her life again.

Lillian loved both boys dearly. She often told me that she felt Cooper was Lance reincarnated.

Prior to my meeting Bono and Cooper, Lillian showed me a precious picture of what appeared to be Lance sitting on Santa's lap.

I remarked, with a warm heart, saying, *"Awe, look at sweet little Lance sitting with Santa."*

Lillian just smiled and said, *"Jenny, that's not Lance. That's Cooper."*

I nearly fell to my knees.

While my dear friend was unable to spend more years of her younger life with her son, she, by divine blessing, was able to spend the rest of her life with his presence.

# Chapter Four

# Two Years of Darkness

Anything without its opposite force is incomplete.

To understand the valuable light within the experiences I am about to share, you should first know why I experienced these situations.

With Archangel Michael as my lead guide since my out-of-body journey, I could always see the divine meaning in nearly every situation.

Precisely seven years after my near-death, out-of-body experience, I had reached a plateau in my *spirit-guided* training.

However, that training had been one-sided, focused on learning the forces and communications of light. I lacked the knowledge of the opposing forces, hence my need to experience two years of *darkness*.

Now, let me clarify that opposing sides are not about good and evil. Opposites are creation itself. Everything has its counterpart; otherwise, unity would not be obtained, and creation's whole would be incomplete.

Through the following experiences, I have learned the darker aspects of life act as supreme catalysts to divine transformation.

*The darkness has a miraculous knack for making much better people out of us by forcing us to seek the light.*

Let me explain through a question. "*What's the first thing people do when they are* suffering, or in religious terms - *when the devil opens a can of whoop-ass on people?*"

They pray to their God Source or a benevolent deity begging to be freed from their suffering situation.

Therein, the so-called malevolent spirit(s) are sending people straight to God.

I've always said religions should adjust their perceptions and teachings regarding the so-called battle between Satan and God. Looking at the human response to suffering, which is often immediate prayer, clearly reveals the battle is between *Humans and God*.

For me, I see darkness, troubles, and sufferings as God's blessed supernatural power at work to dissolve our corrupt ego. As the perfect divine design, the supreme consciousness of Source God ensures that any ego that stands in the way of divine truth and illumination be transformed.

As you will read, my two years of darkness were exquisitely laid out with powerful forces from beyond and two back-to-back relationships, which catalyzed me to embrace divine consciousness - and not just for myself, but for all involved.

I was grateful to have experienced all of it because, in the end, I stood with the most profound, immovable relationship I have ever had with God, life, and the divine guides.

## Head's Up

One evening, I was standing at my window watching a beautiful sunset. At that time in my life, I was peaceful, in perfect flow with my spiritual self, and my life was spiritually steady.

That is, until Archangel Michael transmitted, *"Now, you will enter two years of darkness."*

Of course, I was not game for this at all. Nevertheless, when I looked out the window and saw a beautiful hawk flying in a massive beam of sunlight, I knew whatever happened would be a great blessing of wisdom.

When I heard the hawk's call echo through the mountains, I knew I would be perfectly led and protected.

So, I threw my hands up in the air and said, *"Alrighty then! It can't be that tough if Michael is giving me a head's up about it."*

Exactly one week later, my time with darkness began with my becoming homeless. I had nowhere to live, so I stayed at a hotel for a few days before a friend came forth and let me rent her summer house.

During that first year of darkness, I abruptly moved six times, initially having nowhere to live in each of the moments. I had to resort to staying at a hotel and my place of business until I was blessed with the help of two lovely friends.

## Midnight Quiet

he second time I had nowhere to live, I stayed at a hotel for a few days.

Late one evening, around 11;45 p.m., I was outside enjoying a beautiful, cool breeze. Then abruptly, I felt an eerie sense come over me as the air changed.

I felt a powerful, hot wind blow through the corridor. I knew there was a spirit presence somewhere close, one I had not encountered before.

As I tried to grasp what I was sensing, Archangel Michael transmitted an order saying, *"Be in bed by midnight. Stay quiet. Stay quiet."*

I was a little concerned. But I had learned by now my guidance is always precise and for a good reason, so I looked at my watch. It was 11:58 p.m.

As I turned around to run inside, the heated wind increased, and time slowed everything down, including my stride. It felt as if I were running through a thickness like you feel when you try to run while in the pool.

Once inside, I grabbed my dogs and jumped in bed. As the door latch slowly clicked behind me, the clock struck midnight.

We sat in the bed, watching the door. There was no sound anywhere. Then I heard what sounded like a massive tornado come barreling through the corridor outside.

I knew it was some sort of spirit being with tremendous force. Then it stopped and hovered outside my door as if it were listening for us.

I knew this spirit being was something beyond anything I could understand. My dogs sat with paws crossed, staring at the door as if they, too, knew not to make a sound.

I held my breath and didn't move a muscle. I had never experienced a spirit like this, so I kept praying silently, *"Please don't let it come in."*

Then I received a vision of this spirit in my mind's eye. It was an enormous dark cloud of dust-like matter with a spirit-being inside it. I could see it hovering at the door, listening for me, and I knew it was actually looking for me specifically.

I swear if *it* had heard me breathe or move a muscle, this experience would have gone a completely different way.

After an awfully long minute or so, I heard the massive wind lift, turn around, and leave the way it came in.

While I could breathe again, I surely didn't get any sleep that night.

I never found out this spirit's intention, and I have no idea why it would seek me.

I did, however, learn to *always* do what Archangel Michael guides me to do! *Maybe that was the point.*

## Black Dust

I was sitting outside at work one day with my eyes closed and my face to the sky, enjoying being with spirit and the sun.

Out of nowhere, the wind picked up and blew dirt in my face, interrupting my serenity. Dusting off my face, I opened my eyes, thinking, What the heck?!

I saw a lot of debris floating through the air. When it fell to the ground, I noticed it was black and crispy.

At first, I thought it was tree bark, but it disintegrated into a fine, ebony dust when I touched it.

As if that weren't weird enough, the black pieces were not falling everywhere. The debris was only falling on me and inside my car's sunroof. *My car was parked 15 feet away from me.*

I realized it was a spiritual message rather than physical material when I unwittingly uttered, *"I guess hell hath just been opened."*

As so happened, I wasn't far off on that statement because my two years of darkness soon followed.

## Devil's Den

At one point during my many abrupt moving situations, I was left with no other choice than to move into an apartment the size of a tiny dorm room.

It was located in a commercial building, right above an antique store, which wreaked havoc on my energy as an empath.

I referred to this place as "Devil's Den" because the energy, people, and spirits there were of dark, evil origin.

A woman who worked there wanted to set me up romantically with a man who had his eye on me. I told her bluntly that I wasn't interested.

Later that evening, in meditation, I felt Archangel Michael transmit, *"Take the relationship."*

Of course, I laughed and said, *"You've got to be crazy putting me in two years of darkness and then add a relationship to that. No way!"*

Yeah, like my bucking, the system carried any weight with Michael.

Well, it unfolded Michael's way. The man interested in me became the catalyst for my first year of darkness the minute he walked through my door.

We eventually became engaged, but after enduring eight months of psychosis blended with addiction, we, to my great relief, became *dis*engaged.

When the relationship ended, I was so happy to have time to rebalance after such a trying year.

I transmitted my gratitude to the divine guides for teaching me so much and resolved that I was *done* with relationships.

All I wanted was to be alone and get back to my spiritual life.

However, I knew that probably wasn't going to happen because I still had one more year of darkness to go.

## Soul Flames

When the second year of darkness began, it came with another intimate relationship.

Thankfully, this relationship was one of the best I have had with a person, but it came with its own lessons, of course.

I had only met him three times before our story unfolded, which was the day he came in for a haircut and asked about my upcoming wedding plans.

When I told him the wedding was off, and I was no longer with that man, he said, *"Thank God, I've been waiting for you to be single."* I knew right then Archangel Michael was behind it.

With both of us being spiritually led in a whirlwind, I moved in with him three weeks later.

Ultimately, our relationship, love, and even physical challenges originated from being twin-flame souls who had opposite out-of-body, near-death experiences.

In my out-of-body experience, I had been taken into the light of heaven. In his, he had been taken into the darkness of hell.

We had an indescribable spiritual bond, and I loved him dearly, but the opposing physical energies were too often making me physically sick.

I did the only thing I knew how to do. I asked Michael for direction.

Fittingly, I moved out *exactly* two years after my journey of darkness began. However, my former beau and I continue to honor our friendship.

## The Lord's Prayer

A friend called on me to assist her in taming a spirit in her friend's house.

Her friend had been energetically held captive in her own home by a powerful spirit presence for over two years.

Finally, the woman broke free, fleeing the house in the middle of the night. She ran out, leaving all her belongings behind.

My friend told her she would pack up her stuff and ship it to her. So, she called me to help.

When I arrived at the property, I didn't feel any presence there that would justify a captive situation. However, I was about to learn just how it happened.

As I opened the front door, I went only as far as placing one foot on the floor before a powerful presence rushed in, grabbed me, and pushed me up against a wall.

The spirit had me pinned to the wall with extraordinary power. Being caught off guard, I was stunned, confused, and couldn't think straight. I looked over at my friend and saw her watching in fear and helplessness.

Then I heard my spirit guide speak within me say, *"You forgot to prepare before entering."*

So, with what little spark of power I had in me, I yelled out forcefully, *"Oh, hell NO, you're not!"* Just as I said that, the presence released its hold enough for me to break free.

As I headed for the door, I grabbed my friend by the arm, saying, *"It's okay. That was my fault. I know better."*

I pushed her outside, shut the door behind us, and apologized ,explaining I had forgotten to prepare.

"Let's just go," she said, with panic. "Forget her stuff."

I said, "No. Don't be afraid. Just give me a minute, and it will be fine."

I proceeded to say prayer and asked that we both be divinely protected before entering the house again. This time, the presence had no holding effect on me.

I stood at the door and transmitted to the spirit, explaining what we were there to do, and assured him I was not there to move him from his dwelling. After receiving his energy, I sensed he wasn't a bad being. He was just extremely over-protective of the property.

The spirit followed us closely as we moved about the house collecting the woman's belongings. At times, he was too close, and I had to tell him to back off because he was making me nauseous. And he did.

About an hour in, he finally joined the rest of the spirits in the kitchen area. We could hear the whole family talking together as if they were right there in body. They did their thing, and we did ours.

Before we left, I just had to look in the kitchen to see if I could *see* the spirit family. The minute I rounded the corner to the kitchen, everyone stopped talking.

I just chuckled and said, *"Carry on! Thanks for letting us do this."* As I walked to the front door, they all started talking again.

We definitely left divinely awakened that day!

## Holy Fire Towel

I received a very unique divine message regarding my upcoming wedding.

The message clearly revealed the relationship would *burn out.*

My fiancé and I were at my friend's house one evening for dinner. We had planned on having the wedding there, so my friend took a keepsake picture of us for the memories book.

Soon after this, my friend called me in complete shock and awe over a mysterious towel she had found in one of the rental cabins she owns.

She told me, *"You need to get over here now and see this for yourself."*

When I saw the towel, I was amazed and speechless.

My friend explained that a minister had checked into one of the cabins and found the towel. She said he brought it to her, holding it as if it were a sacred artifact.

In awe himself, he said, *"The markings on the towel are sacred and represent the fire of the Holy Spirit."*

Symbolic images had been meticulously burned into the white towel, one of which was an exact copy – I mean *exact* – of the photo she had taken of my fiancé and me recently at her home.

There was also a symbolic message burned into the bottom of the towel. It said, *"In vii u Domini,"* which I learned means *"God is your dominion."*

As if that weren't enough, the towel also had three trinity markings on it and two interlaced gold rings.

Interestingly too, everyone was amazed that the charred cotton didn't smell burnt. Instead, it had a *sweet,* floral smell.

As we stood outside discussing the possibilities of this sacred mystery, I concluded it was a *soon to be revealed* divine message and pointed my finger up to the heavens.

At that very moment, a beautiful, blue dragonfly landed right on my fingertip.

That dragonfly spirit sat on my finger, literally watching me. Even when I moved my hand while talking, it stayed right there on my finger.

This spirit had no intention of leaving me. I had to lovingly guide it off my finger onto a branch so that I could go home.

Divine truth had been revealed. The planned wedding went up in flames a few months later.


Like the dragonfly, I was lovingly guided to a new branch.

## Death Grip

Dark spirits are often drawn to people who drink alcohol or use mind-altering drugs. This was one of those situations.

My fiancé, at this time, was wasted, sleeping soundly next to me one night. I, on the other hand, was wide awake along with the dark spirits that plagued him.

As I lay there feeling a heavy pressure engorge the room, I suddenly felt *something* climb up on the end of the bed.

I looked down at the foot of the bed and saw what I call a reaper creature, which is a spirit creature that comes to prepare the way for death.

It sat on the end of the bed, peering at my fiancé with deep intent. It then looked over at me, and I heard it say, "Not here for you."

*Phew, was I relieved!*

It crawled up and over my feet and onto my fiancé's leg before disappearing *into him*.

I thought to myself, *Oh, hell no. No relationship in the world is worth this!*

Then a sickly, putrid smell blew through the room. I recognized the putrid smell was coming from my fiancé's body, which was blazing hot. I became sick to my stomach.

When I heard my fiancé – *or the creature* – snort and growl, I heard a spirit transmit, "Leave. Get up. You gotta go."

Shoot, that spirit didn't have to tell me twice!

I was outta there!

Nonetheless, when I tried to get up and leave, I couldn't. I was being pulled back by what felt like a death grip.

At this point, I felt waves of dark energy moving through the room, and the bed began to move. That was all I needed to *giddy up and go*!

I gathered all my power, broke free, and got the heck out of there - and that included the relationship.

## Smoke and Mirrors

At the end of the first year of darkness, the second phase began with mysterious messages being drawn on my bathroom mirror.

I noticed every time I stepped out of the shower in the morning, the steam on the mirror revealed symbolic drawings much like petroglyphs.

I tried wiping the mirror clear, but the drawings would always mysteriously re-appear. I figured they must be important, so I began analyzing them.

A new drawing would appear every morning, and it was either a message revealing daily guidance or a warning of what the day would bring.

By day's end, the mirror messages proved themselves to be eerily accurate. This communication went on every single day for about two weeks.

The last image I received was an unbelievably detailed glyph revealing what I would experience in my second year of darkness.

Having all that behind me now, I can tell you that year took place *exactly* as the spirit had drawn it on the mirror.

## Mountain Man

My boyfriend, who was also intuitive, for some reason did not want me to go on a hike with the dogs one day. Of course, I did anyway.

The dogs and I began walking toward an old mining shaft on the mountainside. I repeatedly sensed I shouldn't go up there. I even heard my inner spirit say, *"Turn around and leave,"* more than once.

With each step I took, I could feel the presence of a dark spirit getting stronger. When I began to feel dizzy and nauseous, that was my indicator dark entities were present. I stopped walking to intuit my surroundings.

I felt an angry spirit presence and received a vision of an old mountain man who had been a miner in charge of the mine shaft back in the 1800s.

I felt he was a mean man in his lifetime, and he had a hatred for dogs. *He was the same in spirit*.

No more did I blink after receiving that vision, my little dog, Kobi screamed. I picked him up and saw that his paw was bleeding, yet there was nothing on the ground that could have cut it.

Knowing this was the spirit's doing, I was ticked off. I said a few colorful words to the spirit, and the dogs and I began making our way back to my car.

On our way, my dog, Dakota, was attacked by wasps that appeared out of nowhere.

I rushed us into the car before noticing my finger had somehow been cut and was bleeding.

When I returned home, I told my boyfriend what had happened. He simply said, *"See, I had a feeling you shouldn't have gone. You need to listen to me!"*

I said, "*Yeah, yeah,*" and of course, gracefully agreed.

# Electrocution Sign

One evening, I decided to wash and groom the dogs.

As I sat on the floor blowing them dry, I felt a spirit presence slowly turn my head, directing me to look at the wall.

To my shock, I saw a slow, steady stream of water *oozing* down the wall. It was just about to drip into the socket where the hairdryer was plugged in.

I immediately yanked the blow-dryer out of the wall and threw it on the floor.

The mindblower here is there was no source of water there. The wall had no plumbing inside it.

The water flowing was thicker than regular water – and, boy, was I glad it was moving slowly!

I sat there for a moment pondering whether it was dark spirits trying to harm me *or* divine spirits sending a message that the energy in the home no longer suited my presence.

Either way, I knew the truth would eventually be revealed. I was just very grateful for the divine intervention!

## Lightning Strikes

The following experience catalyzed the ending to my two years of darkness training.

As an empath, I become physically ill when dark energies appear through people under the influence of spirit entities, drugs, alcohol, or anything that negatively alters the mind.

This was happening too often with my boyfriend, and in our home, so I asked the divine to show me the way one day.

A few days later, I was getting in my car to head home on a clear, blue-sky day when a bolt of lightning came out of nowhere and struck just above my head.

It was so close that I felt the electricity in my body. I went deaf in my right ear, my eyes swelled, and my heart stopped, feeling like it swelled up too.

There was not a second between the next bolt hitting. Knowing things come in threes, I quickly jumped in my car to get out of the line of fire.

While driving home, wondering what that was all about, I heard Archangel Michael transmit, *"The Angel of Lightning is your message."*

Then I began hearing the lyrics *"Little Red Riding Hood, you're everything the big bad wolf could want"* spoken through my sensory system.

Then, as confirmation, I had to hit the brakes because a wolf, running scared, ran right in front of my car. Next, I heard, *"Wolf in sheep's clothing. Wolf in sheep's clothing"* being spoken.

I concluded that all these signs were a message that my home would be blown down, yet again.

I began feeling weaker and had difficulty seeing and breathing, so I pulled over to let the lightning effects wear off.

When I looked in the mirror, I knew something serious had happened because my cat-green eyes had turned to a dusty blue.

I recalled the last time lightning struck so close to me, my extra-sensory abilities enhanced. I figured *it is what it is,* and drove home.

After being shown all the *signs*, I knew the evening would likely be unenjoyable, but I didn't know to what extent.

As I put the key in the door, I paused as I felt Archangel Michael's presence.

He transmitted, "*Enter, and you enter the gates of hell.*"

I was clearly aware that I was being given the choice to enter and fight or flee. I sincerely pondered just getting in my car and leaving.

But, I figured since I had Archangel Michael by my side, warning me, he already knew exactly what would happen. I also had no doubt I would be protected.

So, I shrugged my shoulders and said, "*Well, okay then. Let's get to it.*"

I entered the house, and after a few red flags, I knew undoubtedly, my time living with my boyfriend was up.

My two years of darkness ended that night.

Again, I moved, having nowhere to go. But I wasn't worried because that very day was actually the last day of my two years of darkness time-frame.

Thanks to good friends, I stayed with them until I found a place to live.


Yay! My two years of darkness were complete - *and well mastered!*

# Chapter Five

# The Communications

*If humankind cannot exceed what they can grasp - then what's Heaven for?*

## The Mentalist

I share this experience to reveal how spirit communication can bring forth comforting blessings to others.

Out of the blue, my friend and I were spiritually guided to open a very unique Crêpe Cafe.

There was no doubt in my mind this was a spirit-driven thing because neither of us knew anything about running a restaurant. Neither of us even knew how to make a crêpe, nor had I ever eaten a crêpe!

Fortunately, I happened to have a friend who made crêpes all the time, so I asked if she would give us a lesson. We spent a total of a half-hour learning how to make crêpes.

Then on the wings of spirit, we purchased space, bought some crêpe pans, and opened the crêperie. We opened on the spiritually aligned "soul's in service" day, 11-11-11 at 11 a.m. - and divine spirit kept us in service for three years.

This was not your ordinary restaurant. We only had three employees. My friend and I were the chefs, and another friend was the waitress. We specialized in organic, gluten-free, fresh, handmade foods and catered to people's unique health needs.

Our menu was undoubtedly unique. One of the dishes we offered was called "The Mentalist." When someone ordered this dish, it meant that spirit would decide what they ate!

I would communicate with the person's spirit guide, and the spirit would direct me on what dish to serve and the ingredients to use. Typically, the spirit muse was one of the customer's family members who had crossed over.

For me, when an order for The Mentalist came in, I was so in my element. For my friend, however, it stressed her out, especially after this experience.

One day the waitress came to me with an order for The Mentalist. At first, I was guided to make a salmon crêpe. Then the spirit transmitting *abruptly* changed the ingredients to a vegetable crêpe with no seafood. I prepared it as directed, and the waitress delivered it.

A few minutes later, the waitress came back and said the patron wanted to speak with me, so I went out and introduced myself.

He and his wife had an odd, serious look on their faces, and the wife said, "The waitress told me that you were first led to make my husband a salmon crêpe."

"Yes," I replied, *"but then I was redirected."*

They both smiled, and the wife said, "Well, I just want to tell you this is amazing and thank you. My husband happens to have life-threatening seafood allergies. He can't be anywhere near fish."

We all laughed with relief and thanked God that I could hear spirit clearly!

On another occasion, when a patron ordered The Mentalist, I was led to make an old-fashioned tuna and potato chip casserole crêpe for him.

As I enjoyed remembering my Gramma used to make that dish, I knew the spirit transmitting was the patron's Mom or grandmother. I was surprised we had all the ingredients, so I knew it was important for this man to receive the dish.

The waitress delivered it, and after a few minutes, she said the patron wanted to speak with me. He had tears in his eyes and thanked me for giving him such a heart-touching moment with his Mom.

He said, *"When I saw the tuna and potato chip casserole, It brought tears to my eyes because my Mom used to make that for me when I was a child."*

He continued saying, *"The minute I saw it, I knew it was my Mom who told you to make it for me. Thank you. You gave me so much comfort."*

I asked him if he had recently had contact with his mother's spirit or had been looking through family photos, explaining that loved ones always appear when we focus on them.

He said he hadn't been able to look through her belongings since she died two years ago, but he had been looking through photos of her the evening before and missing her terribly.

In that moment, I knew exactly why we opened the Cafe.

Anything we do "out-of-the-blue" or "against the norm" - doesn't come from us. *It comes through us from Divine Spirit.*

## Crash

A friend of mine asked me to assist with a spirit presence who had been negatively communicating with her granddaughter.

I connected with the spirit and, frankly, found him to be quite an ass.

After going back and forth in a power play, I told him he must leave the girl alone and leave the house immediately. He did not appreciate my interference and gave me a hefty fight.

To break the connection with him, I got in my car to leave the premises. However, he continued his power-play.

After a few minutes of playing the *who-is-stronger* game, I said, *"I'm done dealing with you!"*

I put my car in reverse, gave it some gas, and all I heard was *CRASH!* I had slammed right into my friend's car.

I hung my head on the steering wheel, spewing some choice sailor words to the spirit before I went to tell my friend what happened.

I knew this spirit felt he had won the battle because I heard him laughing. I transmitted to him, *"You may think you've won this one, but it's over now."*

I'm not afraid of tattle-telling at all, so I called upon Archangel Michael to deal with him and went on my way.

My friend's granddaughter thankfully did receive relief from the nagging spirit.

Of course, I gave him a cocky little shout out saying, *"Nana-nana-boo-boo!"* to remind him of the Angels limitless power.

# I'm Busy

I adored my Gramma, my Mom's mother. She raised me during my teen years, and she was my best friend.

I was in my early twenties when she crossed over, and I missed her terribly – *still do.*

I tried communicating with her for years on end and didn't hear a peep from her. Finally, I heard her transmit a message to me one day. As she quickly flew by, she said, *"I'm busy."*

That's it! Just, *"I'm busy."* I thought, how in the heck can she be too busy to communicate with me? I was a little hurt. Eventually, I laughed it off because this "I'm Busy" business went on for 20-plus years.

I couldn't understand how I could communicate with spirits I had never met, such as the divine council, missing persons, strangers, artists, and animals, but not her.

One year, after my near-death, out-of-body experience, a friend of mine held a "spirit communications" class at her home to help intuitive people master their sensory abilities.

We all sat on the floor with a pad and pen in hand. We then drew a participant's name from a bowl and had to communicate with that person's spirit guide.

Once we received the message from the spirit, we would go around the room and share the transmissions. I drew a group member's name and received a beautiful vision and message of love from her great aunt in Italy. The same group member drew my name.

She said, *"Well, I didn't do as well as you did. I couldn't receive anything from your spirit guide. All I heard was, 'I'm Busy!'"*

I burst out laughing and just shook my head. I told her she did better than she thought and proceeded to tell her that was all my Gramma *ever* had to say to me.

Puzzled, I asked my friend if she knew why my grandmother would be too busy to communicate with me.

She explained it quite simply - saying, *"Spirit guides can't communicate with you until you are ready to receive them, and to do that, emotions and judgments have to be out of the way."* Finally, I understood.

After a bit of practice moving emotion and judgment out of the way, I received my first full communication from Gramma.

## Finger Hold

One day, I sat inside my car, in a meditative state, receiving spiritual direction on treating my dog, who had cancer.

As I stepped out of my car, I was still connected, sensing, and listening to what was being sent through me, so I was not grounded in the realm of physical consciousness.

I walked to the trunk, got the dogs out, and shut the trunk. As I started to walk away, however, I was suddenly yanked backward.

This, of course, snapped me out of my higher-minded state into physical awareness. It was then I saw the problem. I had slammed my index finger in the trunk. I just stood there trying to figure how I would open the trunk because the latch was too far away for me to reach it, even in a full stretch.

I thought *I cannot believe I have to stand here, stuck to my trunk for thirty minutes until my client arrives!* However, since I miraculously felt no pain, I finally concluded this higher-mind stuff was quite powerful. I might as well put it to use.

I meditated for a moment and asked the angel guides to help me release my finger. Then magically, I became a contortionist and opened the latch.

The finger was broken, and of course, it went through the physical symptoms of swelling and bruising, but after a bit of energy work and prayer, my finger was as good as new.

I knew right then my higher mind was the only medicine I would ever need.

## Artists Live Too

Artists typically appear to those who are creative with heightened sensory systems because their energies creatively flow the same way.

Spirit beings typically communicate to help divert suffering and/or prepare us for the next evolutionary shift.

The transmissions from the following Artists are provided to do just that.

**Steve Irwin** *(a.k.a. Crocodile Hunter)* - While I never met Steve personally, like so many people, I loved his personality.

About two weeks after Steve's bodily death, his spirit presence transmitted a message, stating, *"I was near and heard everyone ache when the accident happened. I saw everyone hurting. This is a tremendous lesson for all the world."*

*"We are the same with Earth, nature, animals, and love. Everything is all planned,"* he continued.

*"My dad is great too! What a surefire way to go (dying doing what he loved most). Family greets you when you come here!"*

He continued to say, *"Oh, yeah, it's great! This is an awesome thing for me. People will just never know how much!"*

**Other Artists** who have transmitted similar messages of being at peace, with family, and still guiding their friends and families were *Jett Travolta, Michael Jackson, and Anna Nicole Smith.*

As you will read next, I was blessed to have received the spirit wisdom of Freddie Mercury from the band Queen. Having died of "AIDs/HIV" complications, more of what he transmitted directly relates to the SARS-cov virus and vaccines, which will be revealed in my next book.

I also enjoyed a transmission from Tyler Perry's (the movie producer) mom, claiming that her pecan pie recipe was better than mine. She even wanted to prove it with a recipe showdown.

Of course, this Georgia girl responded to her, saying, *"Bring it on, little momma!"*

## His Rhapsody

I am very particular with what I involve myself with when it comes to watching movies and listening to music because I receive spirit energies so easily.

I avoid a lot of media for this reason. However, every so often, I am spiritually led to watch or listen to receive an important message.

One evening I was spiritually guided to watch the movie "Bohemian Rhapsody" about the band Queen and lead singer, Freddie Mercury.

The actor who played the part of Freddie did it so well, I sensed Freddie actually merged with him while shooting the movie - and even afterward at times.

Not to my surprise, I felt the spirit energy of Freddie appear.

After the movie was over, I tried to sleep but couldn't. I kept being nudged by Freddie's presence to receive a message, so I got up, and into receiving mode, I went.

The first transmission I received from Freddie was that he has been communicating with his family all these years.

He also showed me a vision of himself being a muse for artists, which explained how the actor played him so well in the movie. He continues to communicate with family and inspire others today.

As he sang the lyrics, *"I want to break free,"* he transmitted detailed information regarding the SARS-cov virus, the vaccine ingredients, and the effects upon the people, which I confirmed through documentation.

In addition, I received a vision showing all the people who died of the supposed Sars-cov virus - actually did not. Being that our cells are encoded with an afterlife "return time," for those who died, it was simply their soul's time to depart the body. They were not physiologically designed to be able to exist in the times ahead.

Freddie also left a guiding message for us to ponder regarding life challenges...

*"Defuse self from the world with music. It's the only way. Each and every experience carries a frequency of sound, which completes an infinite mystical melody in the end. This is the life experience... good thoughts, good words, and good deeds."*


Even though I cannot read music, Freddie repeatedly showed me a *healing* sequence of notes that were to be played on a piano, noting that at the end of each frame, the final tone echoes into the next.

I found the music to be soulfully moving when a friend played it for me. Intuitively, I feel this musical pattern is meant for musicians and/or songwriters as a pathway to inspire them, connect them with the spirit world, and activate their muses.


Give it a try. You might be *awakened* to something out of this world!

## Dad's Call into Light

I met Jennifer over a decade ago.

I knew she was a free spirit and spiritual when I met her, but I had no idea to what extent...*until my dad passed away.*

The week of Dad's passing, Jennifer communicated with my dad's spirit.

She said, *"Your dad came forth and showed me he was going to be entering into the light. He has accomplished all he agreed to do with all the family. He is showing me March 23 as being his last call."*

She continued to say, *"This means that will be the day he will ascend and go into the light."*

When I received this message from her, I thought March 23 was weird because my birthday is March 22. I felt that whatever would happen would be on my birthday.

Well, the morning of my birthday, I woke up and went out on the deck.

This is what I saw...

I thought to myself, *I knew it was going to be the 22nd!*

The next morning, March 23, I woke up, stepped out on the deck, and saw this...

Unbelievable! Dad entered the light on the 23rd, *just as he had said.*

## The Death Tree

My fiancé and I went to look at his friend's property as a consideration to purchase.

As we drove down the road toward it, I started to feel heavy energy, and an air of upset came over me. As we turned into the driveway, I became extremely dizzy and knew a spirit presence was at this property.

When I stepped out of the car and began walking, I suddenly couldn't breathe. It felt as if someone were choking me, so I bent over, trying to get air.

I sensed there was death and destruction all over this land.

When I stood upright again, it was as if someone had turned my head for me to look at a specific tree. As I gazed at this tree, my empathic senses became outraged.

At this point, I didn't know what was happening. I told my fiancé, *"If we get this property, the first thing we're doing is cutting down that tree of death."*

We returned home, strangely exhausted, I had to lie down. When I did, I received a vision of why I was led to refer to the tree as *the death tree.* It was the tool used to murder a young man.

The spirit of a man named Willie came forth, revealing what happened the day he died.

It was like watching a movie as he showed me a vision of himself hanging from that tree with a look of absolute horror on his face. The horrific sight jolted me out of bed, gasping for air, with tears in my eyes.

Although this scene was too disturbing, I knew it was important and necessary to see. So, I balanced myself again and continued receiving his transmissions.

I asked his name, and he transmitted, *"I was Willie."* He looked to be in his twenties when this event happened.

He began showing me the scene again. The event took place in the early 1900s when evil people were hanging people with dark brown skin.

*I say "brown" because humans are not black, white, red, or yellow-skinned. Except for a handful of albino, charcoal, sun-burned, or liver-related, yellow-skinned people, we are all, in fact, various shades of brown.*

Willie showed me a group of six men. Four men did the deed while two watched. One of the spectators cheered them on, yet the other man knew it was wrong.

These murderous men blamed Willie for stealing, which he didn't do. I watched the entire event as if I were right there. Willie begged and pleaded with them, promising them that he did not steal.

Willie transmitted, *"It was the uncle of the man who owns the property who wanted the hanging."* I was sick knowing the men who killed him were family members of the man who owned the property we were planning to purchase.

Sadly, Willie showed me the whole torturous scene. It was all for the men's sick entertainment.

Then I heard a bell ring off in the distance, and Willie transmitted, *"They rang a bell when it began."*

Willie showed me the look on his face when it started. *I will never get that image out of my head.* Even now, writing this experience, my eyes fill with tears.

I transmitted to Willie how deeply my heart ached for him. I prayed for the divine to bathe his spirit in the greatest love and let the memory of what these men did to him leave him.

Willie then showed me one more vision of being beaten on the left side of his head before the hanging. The men were all laughing, except the one who knew the truth.

I could not bear any more. I apologized to Willie and ended the connection. I was so filled with heartache and anger I had to go outside to walk it off.

I concluded the only thing I could do for Willie was not to support that family by purchasing the property. When I went back inside, I told my fiancé, *"No way in hell will we buy property from that evil family."*

I then shared everything Willie transmitted. My fiancé turned as pale as a ghost with a look of shock on his face.

He wasn't shocked by what I had said. He was shocked that I knew the details so clearly.

*"Jen, about a year ago,"* my fiancé said, *"the owner of that property told me about his family hanging a man from a tree there. He said he saw the man hanging in the tree, and they had hanged him for stealing."*

Immense anger and passion welled up inside of me. I yelled out, *"They lied! Willie was innocent and didn't steal anything! Those sick bastards murdered him for their own entertainment."*

Just as I said that, all the electronics in my house started going haywire. I knew it was Willie's presence trying to detour my scathing emotions.

While I slept that night, Willie came to me in a vision and transmitted, *"Thank you for setting me free."*

I woke with tears in my eyes, knowing that just revealing the truth and acknowledging the event gave his spirit some sense of freedom.

He lovingly stayed present with me for about three days to help free me from the visual trauma of what he showed me. I missed him when his presence faded away.

Seven years later, I was outside gardening at my workplace. I had my head down when a man walked up and said, *"Hi."*

I started coughing harshly as I raised my head to look at him and return the greeting.

When I saw his face, I gasped. I was speechless. This man who appeared out of nowhere looked *exactly* like Willie!

Stunned, I gathered myself enough to shake his hand and say, *"Hi, my name is Jennifer."*

He shook my hand and said, *"It's so nice to meet you. My name is Willie."*

Now, I don't know how all the mechanics in the spirit world work, but I can tell you, I was overcome with profound love knowing that God and the spirit world are indescribable perfection.

It turned out I was able to enjoy the blessing of Willy's company a few times before he once again departed.

## Not Blessing Me

For those who don't know me personally, I'll give you a heads-up... I tend to get a little jacked-up when people try to put limitations on God, nature, and the divine.

One day, I was spiritually guided to go to a church, which is the only time I ever go to church.

Sitting in my pew, I listened as the priest called people up to receive communion. He said, *"If you are Catholic, you can come up and receive the sacrament. If you are not Catholic, cross your arms over your chest to receive my blessing."*

Well, I nearly jumped out of the pew with complete disgust.

I took a moment to meditate and calm myself. Then I transmitted to Archangel Michael, *"Did I actually just hear that man separate people from God?! As if he has the almighty power to choose who can receive Jesus or not?!"*

As I pondered the priest's position that only *a member of the Catholic Church* is worthy enough to receive the symbolic blood and body of Christ, I adamantly resolved there was no way I would go up there.

I silently thought, *"Pfft, that man was not going to bless me with what he had running through him!"*

Suddenly, my temper went silent when Archangel Michael transmitted, *"Go. Walk up."*

Hearing that, I chuckled, snatched my head to the side, and said silently, *"Pfft! No way!"*

Now, I have had enough experience to know that whatever Archangel Michael transmits will take place. He's had enough experience with me to know I would put up a fight. While I battled a bit, I eventually agreed, knowing I would receive some sort of awakening.

I transmitted, *"Fine. I'll go, but don't let that man bless me. You block whatever he puts out."*

So, up I went with my arms crossed over my chest. I watched as the priest looked at those before me straight in the eyes. He spoke his blessing and then placed the wafer in their mouths.

However, *when I walked up,* he didn't look at me. He immediately put his head down and began playing with the wafers in the bucket. I saw that his lips were moving, but I didn't hear a word of his blessing. He then put the wafer in my hand, not my mouth.

I chuckled and went back to my pew, thanking Michael for not letting him bless me and for allowing me to experience the absolute divine truth.

That truth, without a doubt, is that it is the divine beings who guide and bless us - not men who stand behind a podium. This applies to all religions, as I have had just as many hypocritical experiences with the Baptist religion.

Bottom line. If you want to be protected from anything, *just ask the divine!*

## Vaccine Sign

My friend was very apprehensive about receiving the SARS-cov vaccine.

Her son, who is in the medical field, suggested she take it.

Although she was still uneasy about doing it, she took the vaccine. Subsequently, she developed an allergic reaction.

When she told her son about her symptoms, he told her to fill out a reaction report with the CDC. In doing so, she had to provide the vaccination batch number.

She pulled out her vaccination card and noticed that the batch number was the same numerals as her birthdate.

She said she got chills when she saw that, interpreting it as a **GOoD** sign, and felt much better about taking the vaccine.

What are the chances the same vaccine batch you received matches your birthdate? *Great when spirit is involved!*

## The Spiritually Abled

James was a forty year-old gentleman living with the late stages of ALS, also known as Lou Gehrig's Disease.

When I visited with James and looked into his big blue eyes, I saw his beautiful spirit. I didn't see his body paralyzed with ALS, his bodily restrictions, or even his sadness. I saw his soul peering through his sparkling blue eyes.

To me, he, like every living thing, needed nothing more than love.

Every time I saw him, I praised his higher intelligence and let him know how blessed he was to be able to use his sensory abilities instead of brawn.

I spent time with James sharing healing touch, prayer, and deep spiritual discussions. He would light up when I visited and forget about everything else.

However, I noticed every time his wife came to visit him, the room would literally turn dark. The light and joy in his blue eyes would instantly disappear, and fear would come over him.

I watched this woman suck the life energy right out of him just by her presence.

James's nurses had said his wife was horribly mean to him. They said she would constantly call him names and tell him how worthless he was.

The nurses even threw her out a few times. After watching her behavior harm James, I focused on increasing his energy to help buffer her darkness.

One day while talking with James, I noticed his blue eyes were unusually bright. He was so full of life.

Then, he blinked, and his eyes turned black. He looked at me with such fear. I knew I had just witnessed his spirit leave his body abruptly. I had a hunch why.

I turned around and looked behind me, and there stood his wife at the door.

I had never watched anyone's spirit actually flee from the body. I intuited that James was so traumatized by her presence, the only way his spirit could cope was to leave.

I knew James would not be with us much longer because, as I've experienced, when a person's eye color changes to black, cross-over soon follows.

James passed over about two weeks later.


His beautiful blue eyes are now filled with love, light, and joy all the time. It was my great honor to have shared time with him and learn just how deeply energy affects a person's life.

# Phoenix Rising

Phoenix was 27 years old, yet his body looked like that of a twelve year-old child. He was living *within* a body that had been diagnosed with Cerebral Palsy.

Phoenix was so frail. He had to be fed with feeding tubes and often needed suctioning just to breathe. His body, twisted and locked up, did not allow him to move his body on his own. And yet, he was a magnificent, beautiful being.

When I went to see Phoenix, a nurse and I walked in together. She said, *"Phoenix, you have someone here to see you."*

He opened his eyes and looked over at me. He then blinked his eyes with intent. I knew he was saying hello.

I sensed he felt hopeless when it came to communicating with people. I told him not to worry about me not being able to understand him.

I explained that I would be speaking with him from within, and if he *thought* of something, I would be able to hear and know what he was saying. I let him know he would not be limited to eye communication, and he could commune with me in whatever way he wanted.

When I explained the benefits of using telepathic, intuitive communication instead of words, his face lit up as if he was smiling.

I knew he understood this way of communicating because that's the only way he could communicate.

The first thought he transmitted was he thought I was a doctor. I chuckled and transmitted to him that I wasn't the kind of doctor he thinks. I then said, *"I'm a type of spiritual doctor."*

After a few moments of pondering, Phoenix expressed relief and sighed. I then heard his spirit transmit, *"It's exhausting trying to get people to understand me using my eyes."*

I told him I was so grateful to be his new friend and reassured him he wouldn't feel exhausted when we talked. He then looked at me, opened his mouth wide, and twisted his face as if he were in pure agony.

He transmitted, *"Please set me free."*

He wanted to be freed from the life of being unloved and alone. He wanted to die and go home, and he thought I would be the one to help him do that.

I began to stroke his forehead softly with soothing energy and said, *"Oh, sweetie, I am not here to help you die. I am here to help your energy feel better."* Again, he expressed himself with a sense of agony.

I said, *"Shhh. You will be okay."* I gently stroked his cold, frail arm and reminded him of the power in togetherness as I held his tiny, weak hand in mine. He began to relax and took a calming breath. Then he let out a sigh of pure relief, and peace moved over him.

After a few moments, he began to express himself and transmitted, *"Am I ever going to be set free?"* He was asking if he was ever going to die.

When I lovingly reconfirmed I was not there to help him die, he understood and began to cry.

As I watched a tear fall down his face, I felt every ounce of his loneliness inside me. At that point, I knew the only thing he needed from me was the only thing he was missing: *love.*

I shifted my energy and surrounded him with motherly love. I gently stroked his forehead and shared the same love for him I have for my own son – just as if Phoenix were.

He immediately relaxed, and his eyes lifted in brightness and surprise. He could feel the energy transferring, and serenity moved over him. That was all he needed to *feel* set free. He knew I would not set him free in the way he wanted, but he was okay with that now.

I had made a prayer bag with herbs and essential oils for him and felt this was the perfect moment to share it with him. I held the bag under his nose, asking him to smell the healing scent.

He closed his eyes, and with all his might, he smelled the bag. I proceeded to tell him that the plants I used in the bag have the power to soothe his spirit.

Then, hopelessness and longing to leave this world moved over his face again. To shift his energy, I quickly showed him a book I had brought for him. It was a book filled with dog pictures.

As I held the book up in front of his eyes to help him re-focus, he transmitted, *"Oh, I like dogs."* His eyes lit up, and they smiled for him.

I turned the pages asking him to smile when he saw a dog he liked best. After a few pictures, he opened his mouth wide and jolted in bed as he laughed hysterically inside.

It was a picture of a silly looking bulldog with big, buck teeth. My heart was warmed as we were so perfectly together in this moment.

I told Phoenix I would hang the bulldog picture on the wall to enjoy between my visits. As he processed what I said and understood I would be leaving him soon, sadness moved over him.

I knew leaving would be a challenge because he rarely received visitors, especially those who commune with his spirit telepathically.

He transmitted, *"People don't do what they say they are going to do."* He didn't think I would come back to visit him. I spoke to him reassuringly for a bit.

When I thought to myself it was time to leave, Phoenix heard my thought. His facial expression changed to a sad, distraught look, so I lovingly stroked his forehead again with calming energy until he relaxed.

As I prepared to leave, I tore the dog picture from the book and told Phoenix his dog friend would keep him company until I returned.

Being unable to move his body without assistance went out the window. Phoenix jolted his entire body toward me with an agonized look on his face.

He stretched out his arm and held my hand with his tiny, frail fingers, and transmitted, *"Don't go."*

We held hands for a bit, and I reassured him I would be back. Then with a heavy heart of my own, I departed - only to return to see his joyful surprise.

# Sensing the Time

Lupe and I spent ten years ascending our consciousness together.

Having many hours of remote viewing skills together, it was no surprise she intuitively knew her time was near.

About a month before Lupe passed, she kept telling me she felt someone was going to die. Typically, Lupe knew who her senses referred to or had some relation to the scene.

This time, she did not. She even asked me if I felt it was going to be her that died.

While I don't recall my response, *I will never forget hers.*

She said, *"I would be okay dying because I would still be able to communicate with you."*

When I heard her say that, I felt an uneasiness in the air.

Then about a week before Lupe passed over, she called me one evening and said, *"Let's make an agreement right now. If I die, I will come to you and show you everything I experience on the other side."*

I laughed, saying, *"How do you know you're going first? I might go before you!"*

*"No, I'm going first,"* she replied, *"but let's agree that whoever goes first, we promise to show the other what we are experiencing."*

We vowed in agreement, and as we hung up the phone, she said, *"Now, don't forget Scary Fairy! I will come back and show you."*

One month later, she passed over.

True to our agreement, only seven hours after her passing, Lupe was once again with me, showing me what she was experiencing in the afterlife.

## Remote Views

The very evening Lupe passed, just as she had vowed, she appeared to show me a vision of what happened when she crossed over.

In this vision relating to when she died, she showed me her soul being elevated above the right side of her body. She was looking down on her husband and the body she was no longer occupying.

She then transmitted, *"The soul's processing is like an astronaut returning to Earth from space. There's a type of decontamination process that takes place when we switch dimensions. I haven't had mine yet."*

She felt something enter the space, and she turned around to look. She then said, *"I was just told that was enough time. I have to go. Be right back."*

I watched her glide back into a huge blue explosion of light. I knew she was entering the healing dimension to begin her soul's decontamination process.

Then within minutes, she showed me what she was experiencing at the moment she was experiencing it. It was as if I was right there with her.

She was standing in front of a masculine angelic guide. He held in his hands what appeared to be a large book or writing pad.

He was speaking to Lupe, giving her a lot of information about her soul's processing and how things work up there. I felt what he was telling her was extremely important.

However, she was more focused on showing me the space she was in instead of listening to the guide.

I transmitted, *"Girl, you better pay attention to what the guide is telling you, so you know what to do!"*

Then when the guide finished speaking to her, I watched her briefly begin to morph into an *old Catholic nun*. I burst out laughing and transmitted, *"See, I told you, you were a nun!"*

She laughed her little Lupe laugh and said, *"I needed healing when I came here."*

I asked her why I felt Archangel Michael's energy with her. She transmitted, *"I merged with him. That's what they do when we are in training. They make two as one."*

Her energy felt powerful, much like Archangel Michael's, so it began to throw off my equilibrium. I asked her to back the energy down a few notches because it was too much.

She tried, but the waves kept coming, so she sent me a laugh and said she was using me to practice on so she could learn how to work with energy.

Feeling out of sorts, I told her she had better hurry up and master it.

She transmitted, *"Okay. I got this! Watch!"*

Well, whatever she was attempting, *she did not have it!*

So I chuckled and transmitted back, *"I will give you another hour to master this, then I'm coming for you!"*

Eventually, thank goodness, she did learn how to work with energy.

It was so wonderful to have our pokey-fun relationship back.

## A Glorious New Life

My friend, Anne, has a sister named Rose, who has been on dialysis for years.

At one point, Rose had crashed with severe complications and was in the hospital on life support with multiple medical issues.

Eventually, she was transferred to a rehabilitation center to recuperate, where she was not doing well. Anne noticed something *spirit-related* going on with her. Assuming she was dealing with an intrusive spirit entity, she called me to see if I would assist.

I intuitively sensed Rose had a walk-in spirit with her who was severely affecting her overall health. *A walk-in spirit occupies the body only for a short time.* These spirits easily affect the weakened bodies of those afflicted with illness, trauma, alcohol, or any mind-altering situations.

My sense of a walk-in spirit's presence confirmed what Anne had already felt. I told her I would do what I could to help move the presence, but I also wanted Anne present because she is a powerful divine healer.

Before meeting Anne at the medical center, I made a healing medicine bag for Rose and prayed over it, filling it with a divine frequency. When we walked into Rose's room, I was stunned. *This was not the woman I knew.*

Rose was sitting in a wheelchair, bent over crying.

Her hand was twisted around a blanket so tightly that her knuckles were white. She was moaning in agony, crying, and pleading as she spoke to an invisible *someone.*

She kept repeating, *"Why? Why won't you let me go all the way through? Please. Oh, No. I just want to go all the way through. Why can't I go all the way through?"* It was heart-wrenching to see her begging to be received.

Her eyes were the color of black, meaning she had crossed over, so I wasn't sure how much I would be able to do. Using the power of empathic transmission, I connected and merged with her soul. I began to see and feel what Rose was experiencing, which was pure emotional turmoil.

I held her right hand and sat down on the floor before her while Anne held her left hand. In that moment, I felt and saw a lingering presence leave her space.

I then asked Rose if she remembered me. It was obvious she did not. I recognized she was caught between worlds. Then, she looked at us with tears streaming down her face and said, *"They will only let me go halfway. They are saying I can't go all the way through."*

I told her, *"Sweety, we are here to make sure you get all the way through. Don't worry. We will get you through."*

Looking at me, she said abruptly, *"Who sent you?"* I was stunned, waiting to receive words to speak. She looked deep into my eyes and asked again, slowly, *"Who sent you?"*

I looked deep into her eyes and replied firmly, with a voice not of my own, and said, *"God sent me."*

*"God sent you to help me?"* she said, cocking her head. I responded, *"Yes."*

Immediate peace came over her. She was now relaxed, and I could see a glimmer of light in her face.

She asked, *"Are you here to help me?"*

*"Yes,"* I responded. *"We are here to help you so you can go all the way through."*

She then looked up into thin air at something *or someone* and appeared to be afraid. She went into heavy throes of wailing repentance. She began crying and apologizing for things she had done against others.

Rose spoke aloud the names of all the people she thought she had wronged and pleaded for their forgiveness. After a break, she calmed down, and I told her I felt she could go all the way through now.

Very comfortably, Rose said, *"Good. So, I will be dead in the morning."*

My response surprised me. I said, *"No. You will have a glorious new life in the morning."*

*"Yes. Yes,"* she began repeating, *"Yes. Yes. I will have a glorious new life in the morning. I will have a glorious new life in the morning.*

Anne and I got Rose situated in the bed, and I handed her the medicine bag. She looked at me curiously and asked, *"What is this?"*

I told her it was a medicine bag I had made especially for her, and it was filled with God's love and energy.

I explained if she ever felt scared or confused, just smell the bag, and the presence of God would make everything better. She began inhaling the soothing scent, and peace quickly overcame her.

I took a quick moment to rebalance myself and then asked Rose if we could pray for her. She agreed, and Anne and I prayed. After the prayer, *something* happened.

Again, Rose gazed up into thin air and began speaking to someone.

She called out to Jesus, who was clearly appearing before her. She began crying and begging for his mercy. This time, she pleaded with him to forgive her for the heartache she had caused others and herself.

Then, crying, she apologized with the most profound passion I have ever seen any human express. She said, *"I am so sorry if I didn't fulfill my purpose here."*

Anne and I held her hand and allowed her to experience the presence of Jesus. Neither of us had ever witnessed the complete giving of one's self to God like this.

Rose then looked up to the ceiling and went blank for a moment before speaking to Jesus again.

She said, so intimately, *"Oh Lord, you are so beautiful. I love you so much. You are so good to me. I love you, and you love me."*

She also thanked him for being with her and helping her in life. Then she paused. I asked Rose what she was seeing, and she replied, *"I see you."* She repeated this statement four times.

Looking behind me, Rose asked, *"What is that behind you?"*

I asked her to describe what she was seeing. She said it kind of looked like a mattress. I knew what she was seeing was a doorway to the afterlife.

Then, Rose went blank again. I knew her spirit had left her body when her eyes turned black, empty, and glossy. Anne and I truly thought we were going to witness her death and cross-over right then.

In a sense, we did. We witnessed the death of the bondage and suffering she held in her spirit.

Then, Rose *came back* and was more precise. She said, *"The Lord told me that he loved me and that I would go all the way through now."*

She continued to talk further and release more, often looking up and praising Jesus. Anne and I were in absolute awe of what we were witnessing.

Rose then began to praise and glorify the Lord, asking him to take her home so she could be with him. She begged to be with him and confirmed that she did not want to live on Earth anymore.

She said, *"I am tired and want to go home to be with the Lord."*

At this moment, we were sure she would be leaving us, so Anne asked her if she wanted any life-saving measures taken should anything happen.

Without hesitation, she said, *"No. I'm tired. I want to be with the Lord. I love the Lord and just want to be with him always. He is so good to me, and I love him so much."*

Then we watched her face light up with childlike joy. She turned to us and said, *"I want to sing a song to the Lord. Can I sing the Lord a song?"*

We laughed with joy and said, *"Yes! Yes, we are sure he would love that!"*

She began to sing a few lines, and then she started crying, saying she had forgotten the words.

Distraught, she said, *"Oh, no. I want to sing to him, but I can't remember the rest. Why can't I remember the rest of the song? I want to sing all of it to him."*

I held her hand and said, *"Ah, sweetie, sing from your heart. Jesus doesn't need words, he knows you're singing love, and that's all that matters."* She smiled, said okay, and began singing again.

Then, a miracle happened.

With each vision of Jesus, each prayer, repentance, cleansing, praise, and love song, Rose began to receive - and her face became illuminated with golden light. This process went on for a bit.

Then the channels switched. Anne had drawn a picture for Rose that said, *"We love you very much,"* and hung it on the wall in front of her bed. Rose was drawn to look at the picture.

Before long, Rose began repeating, *"We love you very much."* She cocked her head to the side and looked confused, stating every word slower and louder until finally, she exclaimed, *"I see it!"* Her face then altered again to a fearful expression.

I asked her what she was seeing, and she said with confusion, *"Something's happening,"* she said.

*"What are they doing?"* She continued, *"They are moving the picture, changing it, like changing channels on the TV. They are showing me."*

Then, Rose stopped speaking, and a look of deep anguish came over her. She began crying and repenting again as she watched the visions within play out. I felt she was watching her life in review as she moved through the rawest, most authentic parts of her being.

Rose then said she saw the golden light again. This time she said the light in the center was much larger. She was confused and didn't know what the golden light was.

*"Rose, God, is in that light,"* I said. *"When he calls you home, the golden light will appear, and you do not need to be afraid."*

Anne and I told her it was okay to go to the light, and we reminded her, *"The Lord said you could go all the way through now."*

*"Are you sure?"* she asked.

*"Yes. Don't be afraid,"* I replied. *"You will know God is there."*

Rose looked up to the sky again, smiled with a peaceful glow on her face, and said, *"Yes. God is in the golden light. I will go into it and go all the way through."*

Again, she looked up and began apologizing and asking for forgiveness. When the moment ended, I said, *"Rose, all is good now. You have been released through the presence of the Lord."*

I reminded her that she was free and didn't need to worry because God was with her. *"The Lord did tell me I was going to go all the way through,"* she reiterated.

Rose began speaking to the Lord with love and praises as we watched her receive, feel, and know the love of Jesus. Then came the sacrifice.

Here is a woman suffering in the throes of illness and pain in every part of her being, body, mind, and spirit. Yet, when the woman in the bed next to her began coughing terribly, Rose put her troubles aside.

From the depths of compassion, Rose immediately prayed for the woman. She prayed, *"Oh Lord, Oh Lord. My sister is so ill and sick. I pray, please help her, heal her, and be with her. Show her and bless her with the choice to stay or go to you - just like you did with me."*

Hearing this, with tears in my eyes, I said, *"Rose, what you have just done is the ultimate, final release. You sacrificed your upsets to love and pray for another - having no thought of yourself. Now, when God calls you, you are completely free to go."*

I walked over to the woman who was coughing so Anne and Rose could have time together. I knew her coughing was a sign that she wanted to say something.

I sat with her, and the minute I held her hands, she stopped coughing. All she needed was a little love. I spent time talking with her, and she told me of her life pains.

I asked if I could pray for her and give her healing energy for her hip and heart. She joyfully agreed.

Having witnessed everything Rose went through, she held my hand and said, *"This is all so powerful. Um, could I have one of those medicine bags?"*

I chuckled because the woman was so dang cute with her question and said, *"Absolutely! I will make a special medicine bag just for you and bring it tomorrow."*

While I blessed this woman with a little love and friendship, when I was leaving, she gifted me beyond measure with the power of spirit as she said, *"I will never forget you."*

Anne and I left both women to rest and receive whatever awakening the Lord had for them. We were not sure Rose would make it through the night, but we knew she was in divine hands.

Later that evening, Rose crashed and was flown to a major hospital.

The next day, Anne called to tell me that a miracle had happened. *"Rose has been healed,"* she said excitedly, *"It's a miracle."*

Anne said that Rose was nothing at all like she was the day before. She said Rose was now peaceful, full of joy, glowing, and she was traveling the hospital halls, sharing the Lord's message with everyone she saw.

Anne also said Rose had not let go of the medicine bag since I gave it to her, and she wanted me to make her another because it helped her so much.

Day after day, Anne called with the same great report on Rose, who is now fulfilling her soul's purpose, sharing her glorious rebirth, and telling everyone about the glories and miracles of the Lord.


Rose did awaken with *a glorious new life after all.*

# Chapter Six

# The Guidance

*It is not mankind who knows all.
It is spirit.*

## Nine Mom Signs

**W**hen I began receiving the unacknowledged signs my beautiful Mom would be passing over, I had a deep inner nudging to go see her.

She called and told me she needed to have heart surgery, so I began making plans to be with her.

I share these experiences with her and her spirit because there were so many pre-guided signs she would likely not make it through surgery.

We are always given signs in every situation to guide and prepare us for challenges. Through my Mom's guidance, I hope you might receive comfort when your loved ones transition to their spirit selves.

## Ask and Receive

The night before my Mom's scheduled surgery, we were texting each other.

Before we ended our conversation, I wrote, *"Watch for signs from Gramma. She's around, and I think she will contact you tonight. Pay attention to your dreams that aren't really dreams!"*

*"You're too much,"* she replied, *"but I love you dearly. Nighty-night."*

That night, I went into meditation and asked God and Gramma to take Mom on a spiritual journey and give her an experience to comfort her.

The next day, I asked my Mom if she remembered having a spiritual experience or a dream.

*"Yes, I did,"* she said. *"It was weird. I woke up and didn't know where I was. Then, low and behold, this voice was coming at me. I thought it was God, but I couldn't figure out who it was. Then, I realized it was my loving daughter with her infinite words of wisdom."* - Sign #1.

We had a great laugh, but my intuition was heightened, so I knew the experience meant something deeper.

## Sensing Goodbyes

In addition to texting, my Mom called me the evening before her surgery.

She said, *"If I don't make it,"* she told me, *"I want you to know I love you so much, sweetie. I've already called the boys."* My stomach sank. I knew she was saying goodbye. - *Sign #2*

When we hung up, I sensed she had no energy left to care what happened. The signs began increasing with each minute.

## Last Meal

Later that evening, she texted me, saying, *"I just had the best salmon, green beans, and risotto for dinner, which I've never had. Delish!"* She sounded so happy. But I heard a voice within me say, *"Her last meal." - Sign #3.*

## White Horses

The day before her surgery, I woke in the morning hearing and singing the lyrics, *"She'll be riding six white horses when she comes." - Sign #4.*

This message chilled me to the bone because I knew it symbolized death. After reading the lyrics to the whole song, I recognized the eerie connectivity to her, the surgery, and her mom - my grandma, who had already crossed over.

I knew in my heart my spirit guides were preparing me for her rebirth. Still, I tried to convince myself that I was interpreting the messages wrong.

## Long Distance Dance

After a long, concerning wait during my Mom's surgery, I received a call saying she was in recovery.

I thought to myself, *"This is the first time in my life I'm glad I was reading the signs wrong."*

Later that evening, I called the hospital to check on her. I heard concern in the nurse's voice. - *Sign #5.*

I hung up the phone and began packing to go be with her. It seemed I was doing things, but I wasn't getting anything accomplished. Then, something came over me. I just stopped. I sat on the couch with an emptiness taking over. - *Sign #6.*

After a few minutes, I fled the couch, grabbed the phone, and nervously called the nurse again. When the nurse answered, she said, *"Your Mom's pulse has stopped. We are trying to revive her now."*

As a vision of white horses ran through my mind's eye, I listened as the doctors and nurses in the background danced around death, trying to revive her. I heard every sound, grunt, and machine as if I were standing right there in the room with her.

Stunned, I told the nurse, *"Please go save my Mom,"* and I hung up the phone. - *Sign #7*

Being so far away, I was helpless. I couldn't do anything but pray and send her loving energy.

I ran to the couch and immediately went into a heart-reviving energy prayer. I sat rocking back and forth, tapping my heart, hoping to send the energy of my heartbeat to her quantumly.

While I began with rhythmic, forceful heartbeats, as if someone were guiding my hand, my tapping slowed and then stopped after a few minutes. Everything went silent, and I heard a voice within say, *"It is done."* Sign #8

Initially, I felt my efforts didn't work, but then, I felt perhaps my heartbeat did pull her through. I went to the phone and called the nurse again. The nurse handed the phone to the doctor. *Sign #9*

My Mom didn't receive my heartbeat. *"I am so sorry,"* the doctor said. *"Your Mom didn't make it."*

When I hung up, I heard a voice say, *"Your heartbeat saw her through crossing."* I knew this, for whatever reason, meant she needed the power of pure love to be with her to cross over - and she received it. *The number nine represents endings and new beginnings.*

I missed my dear Mom terribly. However, I knew that our relationship was not going to end. And, it didn't. The relationship I have with my Mom now, in spirit, is exquisite and beyond what any physical relationship could ever offer.

## Raiding the Fridge

My Mom's second husband, Lee, experienced a memorable moment with my Mom's spirit not long after she had crossed over.

*"I heard your Mom in the kitchen one night, knocking around in the refrigerator,"* Lee recounted.

*"She was getting food like she always does and woke me up - like she always did."*

I asked him if he told her to do it quietly, and he said, *"No, because I didn't want to get yelled at!"*

I laughed because Mom absolutely would have yelled at him.

Then I asked him if he got up to look.

He said, *"No. I knew it was her."*

## A Creative Viewing

When my family and I were pondering funeral arrangements for my Mom, her husband Lee and my brother were the only ones who wanted to have a viewing and funeral.

The family eventually decided on cremation. However, a mysterious type of viewing still took place - but only for my brother and Lee.

Lee said that morbid pictures of my Mom lying in the hospital bed had been mysteriously texted to him from my Mom's phone.

Yet, her phone was at the hospital and had no charge. He told me that somehow the pictures were then forwarded from his phone to my brother.

Lee said the photos were awful, and he wasn't sure if they were taken before or after she passed, but she looked as if she were dead.

This was very upsetting for my brother. When he received the photos, he called Lee, asking him why in the hell he sent him pictures of Mom looking like that.

Lee told my brother he didn't send the images and that the photos had been sent to him first.

We all knew that somehow Mom made sure her husband and my brother got their viewing, and this experience was her way of giving them a chance for closure.

## Last Birthday Card

One evening after my Mom had crossed over to the Great Beyond, I was going through all the birthday cards she had sent me through the years.

My Mom always found the most beautiful, expressive, heartfelt cards. I thought how much I would miss receiving them. With a heavy heart, I realized I would never receive another birthday card from my mom again.

Then, it dawned on me that she hadn't even sent me a birthday card this year. My birthday had passed by three months ago. I was surprised because this was the first year *ever* she had forgotten to send me a birthday card – *or so it seemed.*

The next day, I stopped by the post office to pick up my mail, and the clerk handed me an envelope.

I stood there stunned and confused as I looked at my Mom's handwriting on the envelope.

The clerk asked if I was okay. I said, *"Um, I'm not sure. This envelope is from my Mom, but she just passed away."* The clerks were intrigued as I shared the many spiritual signs my Mom had been giving me.

When I returned to my car, I opened the envelope. I could do nothing but hang my head in awe and love.

There in the envelope was a birthday card from my Mom.

My sister-in-law said she found the card on my Mom's desk, sealed and stamped after she had passed, and she felt she should mail it to me.

Now, my Mom *just happened* to forget to mail my birthday card...

It sat on her desk for three months...

My sister-in-law *just happened* to find it and mail it at the precise time...

For me to receive it the very day *after* I thought I would *never* receive another birthday card from my Mom again?!

*Pfft! Don't tell me spirit doesn't run this world!*

## Her Scent

The very night my Mom crossed over, I was sitting on the couch writing. Suddenly, my entire condo filled up with the scent of her favorite perfume, *Toujours Moi.*

I just smiled and put my pen down, remembering how beautiful she was and how good she always smelled.

My brother came to visit me that same week. He mentioned he would have loved to have a bottle of Mom's perfume. I said, *"Me too, but I doubt anyone saved her bottle."*

That same week, My aunt had given me a few boxes of my Mom's belongings. That evening, I decided to go through the boxes.

In absolute awe, pure joy, and gratitude, the first thing I unwrapped was my Mom's bottle of Toujours Moi!

I told a friend of this magical experience, and she made this moment even more special for me by informing me "Toujours Moi" is French, and it means *"Forever Me."*

*How beautifully appropriate.*

## Still Dancing and Walking

One evening, my youngest brother was sitting outside gazing at the sky after our Mom had passed over.

Thinking about her and missing her terribly, he was blessed with a heart-touching confirmation that Mom was alive and well.

He texted me, saying, *"I just watched a cloud shape and change into a woman belly dancing. I knew it was Mom."*

Our Mom used to belly dance, and as children, we always got a kick out of her wiggly moves.

My other brother also shared a spiritual moment he experienced with our Mom after she had crossed over.

*"Mom visited me last night in a lovely dream,"* he said. *"We were walking down the boardwalk in the Keys with Bette Midler's 'The Wind Beneath My Wings' playing."*

Being the big sister and always watching out for him, I knew this message had a deeper, more profound meaning for my brother.

Not only did our Mom love Bette Midler, she always loved walking arm in arm with my brother.

The last time the three of us were together, my Mom wasn't feeling strong that day. So, my brother carried her purse, held her hand for stability, and they walked together.

I remember walking behind them, thinking what a precious sight it was to see a son holding up his Mom in her time of need.

*He was the wind beneath her wings.*

For some reason, I decided to take a picture of them walking together that day.

Little did I know then, that day was the last time they walked arm in arm - *or so it had seemed.*

Now, they can walk together anytime they choose.

However, now, she is *the wind beneath his wings.*

## Helpful

This experience reflects just one of many ways those in spirit help us through challenging times.

Having to comply with business sanitation changes due to SARS-cov virus, I spent an entire day trying to find sanitation products so I could reopen my salon. Every store I visited was out of stock. I began to worry about having to close my salon again if I couldn't get sanitation supplies.

When shopping at the natural health store, I noticed a man near me who was terribly sick. He was coughing all over the place. I heard him say as he was talking on the phone, *"I don't think I have covid."*

I immediately felt my Mom's presence swoop in like a wind and guide me to walk down another aisle to avoid him. I then passed by two women talking about making effective sanitizer out of liquor, so I joined their conversation.

Not only did I get the sanitizer recipe, but I witnessed my Mom speak through the woman as she said, *"This is nothing to play with. You must be careful."*

Those words were exactly what my Mom said to me a few days before she passed. In life, and clearly still, in spirit, she was concerned about me getting sick.

Had I not been in that specific store at that precise time and led away from the sick man, I would have never been guided to the aisle where the women were conversing and received their knowledge.

I responded the same way I always did, without worry, and thanked her for still guiding me and being such a good Momma!"

## Motherly Guidance

I had received a warning transmission from my Mom for my brother and sister-in-law one day and shared the message with them.

My Mom transmitted that she didn't want them drinking alcohol. She wanted them to keep their minds clear to receive her guidance so they could stay safe regarding the SARS-cov virus.

The next day, my sister-in-law called me giggling and amazed at an experience she had just experienced with my Mom. She said, "Your Mom wasn't kidding about the no drinking thing!

She continued saying, "I was out shopping and decided to grab a bottle of wine. However, when I got home and looked in the bag — no wine!

I realized I must have left it at the store and thought about going back to get it. But, knowing it was your Mom's doing and that it was important to her, I let it go."

My sister-in-law said she knew Mom was with her while she was shopping. She said she could feel my mom directing which establishments to enter and avoid as a way to keep her safe from viral exposure.

Although my sister-in-law really wanted her wine, I was so touched knowing she was more fulfilled by Mom's guidance.

The following week, it was my turn. While I had a whole day of shopping planned out, mom nixed most of it. She led me to call each store before I entered to ensure they had what I needed. I had no doubt she knew who was infected and who wasn't.

## The Eye of "MA"

My Mom passed over three days before my youngest brother's birthday. I can only imagine how this upset both him and Mom.

During my meditation, Mom transmitted, *"Tell him to pay attention to the signs on his birthday. I want to give him a personal message and life direction as a birthday gift."*

Later that evening, while I was making pancakes, my Mom came through. She was not a happy camper and had some good old-fashioned, *ticked-off Momma* energy flowing.

I laughed and shook my head because I knew my brother had been drinking alcohol and disregarding her previous message. Therein, he was incapable of paying attention to her presence and signs.

I transmitted, *"So, Ma, did you have fun with him today? Did you see what he did?"*

*"Oh, yes!"* she responded. *"I'm watching. I see everything."*

As the eldest, I took a silly moment to revert to my childlike heart. I burst out laughing and did a little dance, singing, *"Ooooooh, he's in trouuuuble. He's gonna get it."*

*"Oh, yes, he is!"* Mom transmitted.

I giggled and shook my head with a side grin because I knew my brother had no idea what the power of Momma could do as a spirit.

I joyfully ate my pancakes, knowing mom would somehow make her presence known.

When I began to clean up the kitchen, *there it was.* As I reached for the bowl's cover, I busted out with a huge belly laugh.

There, stuck to the lid, was a plastic *"googly eye."*

Not only was the eyeball not on the lid when I pulled the bowl out of the refrigerator, but I also had not one thing in my house with googly eyes!

I knew my Mom planted that eye on the lid as an undeniable confirmation that she *was* watching and she sees everything.

Of course, I shared this experience and message with my brother, telling him he'd better watch his P's and Q's.

This takes the age-old saying, "*Mom sees and knows all,*" to a whole new level!

I now wear that googly eye on my necklace as a cherished reminder of her presence and perfect guidance.

## My Heartbeat

I was reminiscing about the eventful day my Mom passed when I had sent her the energy of my heartbeat.

As I felt her presence appear, I said aloud with a loving heart, *"Mom, I tried so very hard to send you my heartbeat."*

She transmitted, *"I know you did, baby. I didn't want to stay."*

At that very moment, I was led to look up at the TV. to see a confirming quote on the screen staring back at me.

It said, *"Each man must decide if they will live or die."*

Mom reminded me of the gift of free will and that somehow, someway, we all choose our comings and goings.

## Lighting It Up

The night my Mom crossed over, she transmitted a message saying, "*I will light up your room.*"

I presumed I would wake up in the middle of the night and see this marvelous shining light at the foot of my bed as I did when Archangel Michael had previously appeared.

Just as she said, I was awakened in the middle of the night to see my bedroom filled with tremendous bright light. The light, however, was not coming from the foot of the bed.

It was a magnificent lightning storm – a lightning storm which I have never seen happen in March. The lightning was continuous, having not one break between flashes.

I gasped at the utter beauty filling my room and then laughed at the heartwarming irony, saying, *"Mom, THAT is absolutely perfect!"*

You might think this isn't all that interesting, but there is a deeper symbolism behind the lightning storm.

I have always *loved* storms - to a *concerning* level. I become completely mesmerized by them, which often puts me in dangerous situations.

This was quite the problem for my parents when I was a child. My fascination with storms always freaked my Mom out, and for good reason.

In my lifetime, lightning has hit so close to me six different times that physical effects manifested. One time, my dad even had to pull me out of the way of an oncoming tornado!

So, Mom lighting up my room with a lightning storm was a perfect memory to honor what I loved and what she feared.

True to my nature and with gratitude, I laid in bed, mesmerized by her magnificent, light show of love.

## Mom's Mystical Girl

I asked my friend Patti, a fantastic artist, to paint a picture for this book. *Our idea* for it was to have a dove flying into an illuminated opening in the sky. However, that is not what the musing spirit painted *through* her.

When she texted me a picture of what she had painted, I was again filled with heart-warming awe. Patti did not paint the dove scene.

She painted a mystical image of a woman with wings instead. A little confused, I sensed this image was somehow a reflection of me, but I didn't know why. So, I asked Patti, *"Did you look at the image? It's a woman with wings!"*

She looked at the image again and said, *"Oh, my! I did not notice that. I just got chills. I thought I was painting the sky and dove image."*

I laughed and told her it was perfect because I knew she had been mused, and I felt the muse who painted the image did it as a reflection of me.

She then said, *"When I began to paint, your Mom was heavy on my mind. I just stopped thinking and painted. After twenty minutes, it was done."*

We were both so deeply touched, realizing my Mom painted this image through Patti as a reflection of how my Mom sees me... *her mystical girl.*

This image is placed at the beginning of the book.

The comical aspect of this image is that even against my Mom's liking, she painted me with dark hair!

## Heads Up

One day well before my dear friend Cindy crossed over, my Mom called, and the first thing out of her mouth was, "*How is Cindy doing.*"

Then, as if she knew, she said, *"I know you love her so much, but I'm afraid Cindy isn't long for this world."*

I thought it was an odd comment but ultimately sensed my Mom's intuition was in play, preparing me for Cindy's crossing.

Soon after my Mom's heads-up call, Cindy went home to the beyond. Eight months later, my Mom also crossed over unexpectedly.

Even though my Mom and Cindy had never met in body, I had a deep sense they would meet in the afterlife.

One evening during meditation, my Mom transmitted that she and Cindy were not working together in the same dimension. However, she confirmed they were both helping with the repercussions of what SARS-cov virus fears did to people's souls.

Through vision, she took me to the moment she and Cindy met each other in the afterlife.

I lovingly watched as they shared a sweet discussion about me - and joked about how oblivious I can be. Our time together faded when I understood what I had always known... *We are all connected.*

# Chapter Seven

# The Preparation

When we perceive our brief time on Earth as our only "Life," we deprive ourselves of our greatest existence.

Soul travel or out-of-body experiences increase as a person's soul nears its day of departure from the body.

As this takes place, people easily access different dimensions of time and space because the spirit knows it will be transitioning soon.

When this happens, I have noticed that those traveling out of body are no longer concerned about conforming to society. That is the freedom the soul needs to depart.

Abiding by what science and society claim to be normal and acceptable can traumatize the soon-to-depart and their process.

Those judging their experiences as crazy, having dementia, and/or giving them medication that subdues them restrict their ability to adjust and embrace death with purity and a joyful spirit.

Out-of-body experiences are a natural part of the life and death process. Out-of-body travel is necessary to ease the soul's transition into the afterlife, and it is paramount so the soul may receive its direction.

Soul travel is also the divine catalyst providing those who will be left behind with great ethereal wisdom.

My friend Cindy experienced a lot of time in the afterlife so she could enlighten us about that which is beyond us.

In honor of her, her soul's work, and her legacy, I share the expanded wisdom she received and shared with me so we might become more aware of the life beyond us - *and ultimately ease our own soul's transition.*

## Hoodjie-Woodjie and the Light

When I first met Cindy, I saw nothing but light in her.

Every time I visited, her face would literally light up with pure childlike joy, and with genuine excitement, she would shout, *"Oh, Hi!"*

She didn't just greet me that way. She greeted everyone that way.

I called her a little ball of light, and she called me *"Hoodjie-Woodjie."* She and her daughter gave me that nickname because I always shared mysterious spiritual experiences with them. She absolutely loved talking about the spirit world!

As her spirit began traveling in preparation to return home to the afterlife, I recognized the tables had turned. I didn't need to share my spiritual experiences with her anymore. She was having her own and needed to share them with me.

Now, it was I who listened to her mysterious spiritual experiences - and I knew why. What she experienced would be important information for us to know about the life beyond us.

One repetitive theme throughout her experiences was that I always showed up at the perfect time to save her from upsetting situations.

One day, when I visited Cindy, she said that her soul travels had taken her to the bus stop again. A few times now, she and other people had been waiting for the bus to take them home.

*"The bus didn't show up again,"* she shared, *"and I was worried about how I would get back here."*

I have often heard people nearing bodily departure refer to waiting for some sort of transportation to come get them.

Cindy said with despair, *"I wanted to call you to come get me, but I didn't have your number or any money to call you."*

She begged me to write my number down and give her some money for the next time - which I did.

*"Oh, no. I don't even remember seeing phones there. What will I do then?"* she said with upset.

I said, *"You don't need a phone to call me."*

I reassured her, telling her she could just ask someone to find me, and they would.

A few days later, the same event happened. *"The bus didn't show up again,"* said Cindy. *"I was getting worried, but then I saw you walking through the group of people coming to me. I guess you got me home because I'm here now."*

At this time, Cindy wasn't comfortable enough to cross over completely, which is why the symbolic bus never showed up.

As part of the divine process, waiting for transport allows the human brain time to become comfortable with leaving the Earth dimension.

Each time Cindy waited for the bus, she became more ready for her transition.

## Happy Me Up

ome of Cindy's experiences scared her, and at times, she felt as if she were all alone.

Often when she was on the other side, Cindy felt she had no one there to help her understand what she was supposed to do.

To help ease her mind, I said on one occasion, *"Don't worry. I will come to you in your dreams, so you know you have a friend on the other side. Next time you feel scared or alone, just yell out my name, and I will come be with you."*

"Really?" she asked. *"You can do that?"*

*"Sure!"* I shot back with a confident grin.

Relieved, yet still a bit doubtful, she looked at me and said, *"Okay. I'll remember you're gonna meet me in my dreams to happy me up."*

I wasn't sure if I could pull off traveling to the dimensions she was visiting, but I figured it couldn't hurt to try. She was already so lonely, and I did not want her to be afraid of the afterlife.

That evening, I meditated and asked the divine for assistance in allowing me to be there for her when she called my name.

When I awoke the next morning, I knew I had been with Cindy, but I didn't recall what we had been doing.

I found out when I went to see her, however.

As I opened the door, she shouted, *"Oh, thank goodness, you're finally here! I have been waiting all day to tell you what happened last night in my travels."*

I laughed, sat down beside her, and listened to her share her experience:

*"I was waiting for the bus again. This time nobody was there with me. It was getting dark, and I began to worry about how I would get back here.*

*I wanted to call you. Then, I remembered you said I should just call out your name and you would come. So, I did. I waited for a few minutes and doggone it if you didn't walk right up behind me and hold my arm! I was so happy to see you.*

*You helped me with something, and then other people started showing up. When I wasn't alone anymore, I watched you walk away to the top of a hill.*

*You stopped, turned to me, and said, 'You see now. Call my name anytime.' Then you disappeared.*

*I woke up this morning dying to tell you that you <u>did</u> come happy me up! I still can't believe you did, but I feel so much better about all of this now."*

As she spoke, I began to recall our otherworldly visit together, but the only thing I could retain was knowing that fear and loneliness are a person's choices. Neither has ever existed.

*Choose togetherness.*

*Always togetherness.*

## Checks and Lavender

On another visit with Cindy, she shared a bit of lovely information about being *over there.*

*"When I was over there at the other place, I wanted to write you a check for something,"* she said, *"but I couldn't because they don't take checks there!"*

I just laughed, and as I sat down beside her, she spouted, *"Oh, you smell good. What's that smell?"*

I told her it was lavender essential oil.

*"Oh yes. That's what it smells like over there,"* she added. *"That smell is everywhere, and it smelled so good."*

She switched gears quickly and told me repeatedly that the three of us *(I, she, and her daughter)* would be going on a *"trip of rest"* together.

I knew this meant she would be taking her final trip to the afterlife soon, and we would all come to rest.

## In Eden

During one of Cindy's afterlife travels, she told me she was very upset because there was nowhere to go to the bathroom over there.

Cindy had a bathroom *"thing."* She always spent a lot of time in the bathroom - not *going*, but just messing around.

She continued to say, *"I thought I had to go to the bathroom, but the only place to go was outside in the garden,"* she recounted.

*"It was so beautiful, just like the Garden of Eden. But I didn't want to go there and mess it up. Plus, I was worried someone would see me."*

I laughed out loud as I had a vision referring to scripture and said, "Well, honey, you don't need to worry about that. If it was the Garden of Eden, no one is there!"

She burst out laughing and said, *"Oh, yeah. I forgot about that."*

## Sacrifice

The day the nurses found Cindy sleeping on the floor, I visited and asked her to explain what had happened that night.

*"I went to a type of holding place,* she said. *"It was a huge building made with white stone and pillars. There were a lot of people waiting to go through the door to the other side. And when you went through that door, everything on that side was peaceful and good."*

She continued saying, *"I noticed the man in charge. He was calling the people who could enter by name, but he was only calling the names of people who knew things.*

*The ones who had not learned - were not allowed to go through the door."*

This upset Cindy very much. She said her heart broke for the people not being able to go in.

She shared much more: *"When the man called my name to enter, I started walking up but stopped and looked back at the people. They looked so sad, knowing they could not go.*

*I thought to myself, it isn't their fault they don't know what they need to know to get in. They were never taught about it. I couldn't bear the thought they would be left behind.*

*Right then, I made my decision. I told the man I would pass up my chance and stay behind to help the young people learn.*

*He asked me if I was sure. I thought about it again and said, 'I'm sure.*

*Then I walked over and sat with the people who couldn't go. All the names had been called, and I watched the door close. Then we all lay down on the floor and fell asleep."*

As I listened to her share her great sacrifice, my eyes filled up with tears of love and gratitude because I knew what she had just done. She had given up her chance to stay in the glorious afterlife to return here and help people learn.

Shaking her head, she said, *"Jennifer, I was shocked when I woke up here this morning. I couldn't believe I was back in my room! I even woke up on the floor in the same position I was in when I fell asleep over there. I just can't believe I'm back here."*

With heartfelt gratitude, I thanked her for sacrificing her glorious time there to come back and help us learn about the afterlife.

With a laugh, I said, *"You know people aren't the brightest things, and we need all the help we can get."*

Cindy shook her head in agreement, saying, with a matter-of-fact tone, *"That's why I came back."*

As she grasped the profound duty behind her experience, she began to feel better.

When I visited Cindy the day after her sacrifice experience, I opened the door and yelled, *"Welcome back, O' Mighty Oracle!"*

She burst out laughing, and I could tell she knew my statement was true.

I then sat down next to her, thanked her for coming back to teach us, and handed her a stuffed bear I had bought for her.

I had attached a note to the bear that said, *"Thank you for sacrificing your cross over so you could come back and teach us. We love you."*

She looked at the bear and spoke to it as if it was a living being. She said, *"Oh, my friend, please stay with me always."* She held onto him the whole time I was there.

Cindy was worried her daughter would think she was crazy and not believe her experience and that she died that night.

When I told her, *"She already knows. She told me she already knew you had died and come back to us."*

Surprised and happy, she asked, *"Really? How did she know?"*

I told Cindy her daughter said she had prayed, asking for confirmation from God. I have never seen Cindy more comforted than in that moment.

She was so relieved her daughter believed her it was as if the final piece to her puzzle had been put together.

Her entire being expressed the energy of - *my daughter believes me. I can go now.*

Cindy then switched gears and asked me in a serious tone if I was writing down everything she was experiencing. I assured her I was.

Cindy spent the last year of her life exploring the afterlife for us - so we could learn enough to go through the doorway ourselves when our names are called.

Her sacrifice and the wisdom she shares with us in this book are her lasting legacies.

## Little Reaper

When the soul is preparing to leave the body, various spirit helpers appear. They come forth to help align the soul with the afterlife, which ultimately helps ease the soul's transition between worlds when one crosses over.

The little reaper animal is a common visitor. These beings typically appear before someone passes over to pave the way for an accident to occur. The accident ultimately activates the death process on a cellular level.

Cindy's little reaper appeared to her one day while I was visiting her.

I was sitting on the floor, rubbing a healing ointment on her legs. We were having a general conversation until she curiously looked over at her desk.

With a confused, concerned look on her face, she began asking *someone or something* questions. *"Who are you? What are you doing? What do you want?"* she asked.

She looked at me and asked, *"Do you see that little thing?"* I asked her to describe it to me. As she did, I knew exactly what it was and what it was doing.

Cindy said, *"Do you see that little animal running back and forth on the desk? It's looking for something."*

Curiously she watched it and then said, *"Wait, now it's looking down at the floor."*

As she looked at the floor, Cindy gasped and said nervously, "Oh, no. It's looking at that big hole in the floor. Oh, no! Where did that come from?"

She became distraught, thinking that she would fall into the hole when she walked around the house.

Even though I knew an accident had already been laid out, It wasn't my place to interfere, so I said, *"Oh, yes, I see him now. He's just a little spirit helper. Don't worry about the hole. It will close when he leaves."*

After discussing this subject for a while, I asked if the animal and hole in the floor were gone. She said with relief, *"Yes. Thank goodness. I don't want to fall into that hole one night."*

Cindy then looked at me and said in a serious tone of voice, and honestly, not a voice belonging to her, *"You must write down everything I say because it's very important."*

I promised, and I did.

After helping her get ready for bed, I sat with her quietly as I listened to her talk with her Mom. She always held her Mom's picture in her hands and spoke with her before bed.

Tonight, Cindy told her Mom, *"I'm ready to go now."*


The nurses found Cindy on the floor the following day.

*She had fallen during the night.*

## Something Better

Cindy wasn't getting much sleep due to her increasing afterlife adventures.

I told her she had to get sleep and suggested she try breaking the interruptions.

"When the spirits interrupt you," I said, "just tell them you are not interested and start singing the song 'You Are My Sunshine.'"

I had hoped that might help break her pattern. To make sure she knew the words, we joyfully sang the song together.

After about a week, she said, "Okay, you have to give me something better than saying I'm not interested - to get me out of the places I go - because it's not working!"

I asked her if she'd had a bad experience.

"No," she answered. "I knew what they were saying was all true, but I didn't want to hear it. I tried saying I wasn't interested. It worked a few times but not now. When I realized it didn't work anymore, I said, 'Doggone it! Now that's gone too!'"

After a good laugh, I said, "It probably didn't work because you needed to hear the truth they spoke to you. Tell me, did you sing the song?"

"Oh. No. I forgot that," she replied, scrunching her nose a little. "See, when I'm in it over there, I forget about things here."

I sensed this was the point when she realized what her soul-self would be doing in the afterlife.

## Out of Body

When I went to visit my darling Cindy one day, she said, "Oh, I had something weird but interesting happen!"

*I saw myself standing on the outside ledge of the windowsill. 'I' was so happy and joyful up in the air. Then I wondered how 'she' got there."*

I knew seeing herself as two aspects *(I and she)* was a clear sign the here and hereafter dimensions were beginning to merge as one.

She asked, *"What was that? How can I see myself in two places like that?"*

I explained she simply had an out-of-body experience, and it's quite common.

*"Well, I like it!"* She exclaimed. *"Why don't we have them all the time?!"*

"Actually, we do," I said. "We have out-of-body experiences every night when we sleep. It's what people refer to as dreams. We just don't normally remember them."

With her child's heart, she said, *"Well, we need to!"*

## The Calling Stone

Sweet Cindy was experiencing frequent out-of-body travel by this time.

While visiting her one day, she told me she heard a voice speaking when she was on the other side.

She said, *"I knew the voice wasn't the right voice. I knew I was safe, but I didn't feel safe hearing that voice. I began to worry about how I would get back home, back here."*

She continued saying, *"I was worried, so they gave me a big stone. It was kind of shaped like a pear or something, you know, with curves. It was green and smooth like porcelain. They said I could use it to call for anything because the stone can do anything.*

*I'm nervous because I can't find it now. I need it to be able to call someone. But then I remembered, you said you would take me home, so I didn't worry about it anymore."*

To comfort her, I reminded her about us being together in her dreams, and all she had to do was call out my name, and I would appear.

Here is where the magnificent awe of spirit comes in. A few days later, one of my clients came to my salon with a gift for me. When I opened it, I was absolutely speechless.

It was a large pear-shaped, green, smooth like porcelain stone! It was the exact replica of the stone Cindy described and couldn't find.

My client said she was led to gift me with it, and it held the power of connection with the spirit guides.

When I showed it to Cindy, the minute I put it in her hand, I watched her gasp, close up, and basically shut down. She just looked *into* it and didn't say a word.

For over a year, I had no idea what type of stone this was. However, when writing this book, I decided to have my friend, a geologist, examine it. He identified the stone as jade.

Jade happens to be used by many tribes and spiritualists for *contacting* spirit guides and ancestors to receive wisdom and helpful assistance.

## Shiny Calling Cards

During one of my visits with Cindy, she shared an experience saying she had been visited by "shiny people." I refer to these spirits as shining beings who bring awareness of the afterlife to those nearing crossover.

Cindy recounted, saying, *"These strange shiny people visited me last night, and they were sprinkling little shiny pieces, like circles, all over me and my room."*

She said, *"I was a little scared and didn't tell anyone because they would think I was crazy. But I know you believe me."*

I reassured her she was perfectly sane and explained it was just a unique spiritual experience, and lots of people have been visited by the shining ones.

When it was time for me to leave, I kissed Cindy on the forehead as I always did when leaving. When I leaned down to kiss her, I saw something sparkling on the floor under her chair.

Smiling, knowing exactly what it was, I picked up three silver, shiny circular pieces.

Showing them to her, I laughed and asked, *"Is this what they sprinkled in your room?"*

Her eyes widened, and she smiled from ear to ear, saying, "Yes! Yes! Where did you get them?"

I said, *"I just picked them up off the floor under your chair."*

Cindy looked at me with the cutest sideways grin I'd ever seen and said, *"See, I told you they were here."*

I laughed, saying, "*You know you're talking to the queen of Hoodjie-woodjie here. I believe every word you say!*"

To help her understand what she experienced, I explained that spirits often leave items as their calling cards; it's their way of letting people know they were present and that people witnessing their presence aren't crazy.

Cindy felt so much better about her sanity when "the proof" revealed her truth. Now she *knew* for a fact that she wasn't going nuts.

I then placed the three shiny pieces in my wallet to show Cindy's daughter the actual proof. They stayed in my wallet for a few days until I showed her. Then they mysteriously disappeared.

Not long after this, I had another interesting moment with the "Shining One's" soon after my Mom passed over.

I was looking through my family scrapbooks one evening. Just as I opened a card I had received from Gramma over thirty years ago, a shiny silver circle, just like the ones I found at Cindy's, fell into my lap.

Now I have opened that card too many times to count through the years, and never has a shiny circle appeared - anywhere.

Comforted, I smiled, knowing we were all connected, and I had a deep sense that my Mom, Gramma, and Cindy's Mom were likely Shining Ones themselves.

Once again, I placed the shiny circle in my wallet to show my friend. Yet, when I opened my wallet to show her, the shiny circle had again mysteriously disappeared.

## Angel Bear

This experience I'm about to share is more of a message than a sign, but it's worth mentioning because everyone needs a forever friend.

As I started to sit down on Cindy's bed one day, she yelled, *"Oh, no! Don't sit on the pig, or dog, or whatever it is."*

I laughed and asked, *"Do you mean the stuffed bear?"*

*"Yeah,"* she said with a chuckle. *"I can't see well. It's some kind of animal."*

We giggled, and I held the bear up to show her. *"Oh, yeah,"* she remembered. *"You gave me that bear!"*

*"Yes, I did,"* I replied and reminded her why I gifted her with the bear; *for sacrificing her cross-over to come back and teach us.*

She remembered that day and took on a look of sadness.

I handed her the bear, hoping it would comfort her. She held the bear in her lap, stroked his face, and gazed at the bear with deep loneliness.

I wanted to break the sadness she was feeling, so I asked her, *"Did you name the bear yet?"*

*"No. What should we name him?"*

I said, *"What about Angel Bear?"*

Hearing that, Cindy's face lit up with childlike joy, and she said, *"Yes! Yep, that's his name!"*

She then looked at the bear as if he were her closest friend in the world and began crying.

*"Angel Bear, my friend,"* she said, *"please protect me and stay with me always when I travel over there."*

My heart ached as I told her, *"Angel Bear will always be with you."*

*"Good,"* she responded. *"I feel much better now."*

## The Other You

One day when I walked in to see Cindy, she looked at me, smiled oddly, and said, *"Oh, hi! It's you today! I know who you are, but what's your name?"*

Thinking she might be a little foggy from dimensional travel, I laughed and said, *"It's me, Jennifer."*

Cindy chuckled and shook her head, saying, *"No, no. I know that, but you're not you - you're the other you today."*

This is not the first time I have heard this from people, so I asked her what I looked like.

She responded, *"Well, you look like you, but there's something different the other you has."*

I was the *"other me"* with Cindy for about a week. Then, one day I walked in, and she laughed and said, *"Oh, hi! Your other you is back now!"*

We laughed and laughed, talking about how exhausting it must be to have two of me.

Then, Cindy looked above my head with a curious look and said, *"What is that you're attached to? There's something attached to your head. It's like strings, stretching up to the sky from your head."*

*"Oh, those keep me connected to the other me!"* I said.

Cindy giggled in response. I found this comment odd because I often feel string-like sensations on my head.

The "other you" reference has a further history.

My ex-fiancé also referred to *the other you* when I had visited unpleasant dimensions during my sleep, which was often the case given his troubling impact on our lives.

I always knew when I had been somewhere not in alignment with my soul because I would wake up flaming hot. Eventually, I learned not to sleep on my stomach as a way to stay out of the unpleasant dimensions.

Early one morning, I woke with terrible arm pain and realized I had been sleeping on my belly. I knew whatever dimension I ventured to during sleep, someone had forcefully been holding me down.

I asked my ex-fiancé why he let me sleep on my stomach and didn't wake me to roll over.

He said, *"I tried, but your other you said to let you stay there for a bit."*

"What?" I laughed and asked. *"Who is the other me?"*

*"Well, there's the traveling you,"* he said, *"and the awake you. It was the traveling you who said let you be."*

By the way, my ex-fiancé and Cindy had never met or spoken to each other.

## Signs of Home

We all knew Cindy's time was near when she began seeing children in her room.

It was a lingering reminder because Cindy's husband also saw children appear in his room before he passed over.

When Cindy told her daughter about seeing children in her room, she looked at her daughter and asked, *"Now, what was it Dad saw before he died?"*

Hearing that question chilled Cindy's daughter to the bone because she knew it was her way of preparing her for her mother's crossing.

The signs were increasing daily. Not long after this exchange, we received another sign she would soon depart when Cindy injured her leg in a fall.

When I asked her how she fell, she said, laughing, *"I was traveling again, and I fell from a tree when I was outside playing with the two boys."*

## Smoky Room

The next sign was when Cindy told me she saw smoke in her room. She said everything was hazy and smoky white, and she could not see through it.

This is a typical sight of the afterlife. However, the white smoke was coming *to her* instead of her going into it - which meant *"the afterlife was coming."*

## Invisible Man

Another sign of her transitioning appeared when she told me she saw an invisible man speeding through the halls. She said he was looking for someone and checking on things.

When he entered her room, Cindy felt the man had found what he was looking for. She said, *"He was moving so fast. No one else saw him but me, not even the nurses he passed."*

When I explained that she saw a spirit, she asked how she could see him, but no one else could. I told her it was because she had spiritual abilities.

She then looked at me, cocked her head, and bluntly said, *"Well, I don't want them! They're a pain in the ass."*

## The Eyes

As I have mentioned previously, one of the most defining signs of having been in the afterlife or nearing cross-over - is eye color.

I went to see Cindy one day and immediately noticed her eye color had changed from her usual light blue to a deep indigo.

Abrupt changes in eye color to darker colors, including black, typically happen when the soul has been detached from the body.

## A Mouthful of Leaving

When I visited Cindy one afternoon, she said, with amazement and relief, *"Oh, perfect timing! You always show up to save me!"*

I asked her what had happened. As she proceeded to tell me, it was clear she *knew* it was time for her to go to the other side.

*"Deep things are happening before I go,"* she shared. *"I can't get the beauty in things here anymore.*

*I need to get my stuff together. Will you make sure I have everything before I leave Friday?"*

She continued, *"Oh, how am I going to get to work over there to help with the water group?"*

The water group refers to the work her soul would be tending to in the afterlife. She had been shown many times in her travels that her group would be helping restore the spirit (water) to the people after suffering acts had been brought upon the people.

Everything she was shown and spoke of happened six months after her crossover, as SARS-cov sickness and the governments destroyed the human spirit.

She continued, *"I don't want to stay here too long. I don't like their ideas here. I get good thoughts over there."*

Then she began pleading.

*"My place is ready. It's time to go,"* she said. *"I've been traveling all day. They have a place ready for me, and they said I could come anytime. I have to go.*

*I'm going to go. I have already canceled things here. I have to go over there now, Jennifer, and I want you to take me."*

Entirely distraught, Cindy then confessed, *"I should have stayed there. I had already made up my mind to stay there. I thought I had plenty of time in my head to think, but then it happened so fast.*

*I have to go there. Jennifer, come on, we're wasting time! I've got to go. I've got to do it. I can't manage myself here."*

I calmed her down a bit by having her take a few deep breaths. I needed the pause too.

She then said, *"When I saw you walk in, it all came together."*

She went on, this time in a quieter manner. *"You have to take me over there. You always come at the right time and always show up to save me when I need help. You must promise to take me there. Please promise. Do you promise?"*

Stunned at what she revealed about the afterlife and her desperation, I promised.

She then said, *"You need to rest. All three of us (me, her, and her daughter) will go together, and we will rest. Let's go on our trip now. Okay? Are you ready to go?"*

Lowering her head, she looked at her hands and said, sadly, *"Oh. I won't be there."*

The three of us often took little outing trips together. However, in this moment, she understood we wouldn't be doing that anymore.

Cindy then began speaking about her friends on the other side. *"We already started celebrating my being home, but no one is taking me there,"* she said.

*"I remembered you said you would take me, and I am leaving when my daughter gets back from her vacation. Please call her and tell her to hurry up and not to go home first, but come straight here - because I can't wait."*

This was the only time in my life I was at a complete loss for words. The only thing I could eventually speak was, *"Everything would be okay."*

She finally became comforted when I told her, *"I will always be there for you. I will meet you in her dreams again, and we will go there together."*

I left that day with my heart dragging on the floor behind me.

*Everyone I've ever met who has been to the Great Beyond longs to get back.*

## Tasty Jen

As Cindy progressed, her experiences fluctuated between the mysterious, scary, intriguing, and comical. The following experience was one of the funny moments.

We were having dinner together one evening, and I was thoroughly entertained at how the *soon-to-depart* saw things. In Cindy's defense, her eyesight wasn't particularly good.

Attempting to pick up the food on her plate to eat, she grabbed my hand and asked, *"What's that?"*

*"That's my hand,"* I replied, chuckling. She burst out laughing and said, *"Oh! Well, it looks so good I could eat it."*

Then she started plucking my arm and asked, *"What's this?"* Grinning, I said, *"Now that's my arm!"*

*"Oh. Your arm might taste good too!"* She said.

After a few minutes, she began grabbing my leg. I burst out laughing, saying, *"Now that's my leg!"* Cindy scrunched her nose and said, *"Oh, no. That won't taste very good!"*

She then leaned to the side to look around me and asked, *"What are those things running behind you?"*

Curiously, I asked her to describe what she was seeing.

*"They're like tubes,"* she said. *"They look like green beans."*

I chuckled, responding, *"Well, you can't eat me, but maybe you can eat those green beans!"*

That was the last time I heard her laugh out loud, and it was our last intimate moment together before she crossed over. I was so blessed it was filled with joy and laughter.

## Knock, Knock

The day Cindy crossed-over, my friend, her daughter, said she had stepped out on the deck to look at the day.

As she scanned her surroundings, she thought to herself, *What color is that?*

It was the darkest, most ominous day she had ever seen. She knew that color of sky was not a good sign. Intuitively, she felt her Mom would be passing on this day; Cindy did, in fact, that very afternoon.

My friend was with her Mom as she crossed. After Cindy had passed, her daughter said she walked outside to go home, and the sky was still that awful, ominous color.

Then, out of nowhere, the dark clouds rolled away, and bright blue skies appeared, and a bright beam of sunlight shone down.

She said it was like a switch had been turned on, and all the gloominess was gone. She knew it was her Mom telling her she was okay and at peace.

On the way home, my friend decided to turn on the radio to fill the silence. The song playing was *"Knockin' on Heaven's Door" by Bob Dylan.*

Again, she knew it was her Mom, letting her know she was safely in heaven.

Similarly, when my dad passed over, I turned on the radio not an hour after the funeral service, and the same song was playing.

Those in spirit know one little sign from them is all it takes to overcome grief - *which is exactly why they give us signs.*

## The Code

The morning Cindy returned to her life beyond, I woke with a very cumbersome, unpleasant feeling.

I had planned on going to have dinner with Cindy after work. As I was driving to her place, her daughter drove past me. She called me and told me Cindy was gone. I thought she meant they had moved her to another facility.

When she confirmed Cindy had passed away, I was stunned and had to pull over.

I took the information in and decided to go visit her anyway. I sensed that in some way, Cindy was waiting for me.

I arrived and sat in the parking lot in silence with a heavy heart. I thought about the many times she asked me to take her home with me, and I always had to tell her, *"I would love to have you with me, but there are too many stairs for you to climb."*

I thought, *well now, in spirit, she can do anything!* So, I chuckled and said out loud, *"Well, Cindy Loo, you can come home with me now! Hop on in!"*

The moment I said that I heard a faint bell begin to ring on the passenger side of my car. It was the same bell sound I heard when Gramma had passed over.

After listening for a few moments, I noticed the bell was ringing in a pattern.

Being a numerological linguist, I knew it was a form of morse code sequences and knew Cindy was sending a message.

After decoding the numbers, I understood her message clearly. Her message revealed she would be communicating God's divinity and infinite totality.

Then she transmitted, "*It is my job. I am going to make the waters (spirit) flow.*"


I can tell you with every ounce of my being, Cindy made the spirit flow in my life. And... All she has shared with us in this book reveals "*God's divinity and infinite totality.*"

## Sweet Potato Soufflé

I spent every holiday with Cindy and every holiday she wanted my sweet potato soufflé. She loved it and always looked forward to my making it for her.

After Cindy's passing, I was reminiscing about a day I decided to mess with her head. As I walked into Cindy's apartment, she looked at my empty hands, confused, and said, *"Um, I don't see anything in your hands! Where are my sweet potatoes?"*

Apologetically, I said, *"Oh, Cindy, I was so busy I didn't have time to make it for you. I'm so sorry."*

Her eyes bugged out, and she puckered her bottom lip, making a sad face. I laughed and said, *"You know I will never leave you hanging. I always make you your sweet potato soufflé!"*

Having hidden the soufflé in my handbag, I pulled it out and surprised her. Her eyes lit up, and she licked her lips like a child in a candy store. This was my favorite part of her. I just loved seeing her childlike energy.

I thought how much I would miss seeing her light up the room. Then, feeling an emptiness - I realized I would never make my sweet potato soufflé for her again.

Right on cue, and to my joyous expectation, Cindy appeared and transmitted, *"Oh, no. You still make it. I'll be there!"*

I laughed out loud, knowing I could expect to find little angel bites in the soufflé next time I made her the soufflé.

*No one wants to be forgotten when they go invisible —*

*And they shouldn't be.*

# Chapter Eight

# Animal Spirit Guides

As ancient beings, animals are our spirit guides.

They existed long before humans and will continue long after.

I have always been one with the animals, so communicating with them comes easy for me. So much so, my friend gave me the nickname *"Elly May,"* reflecting the animal-saving girl from the Beverly Hillbilly's TV show.

I know animals are not just animals. For me, they are spiritual beings; *divine guides, guards, and guardians* sent to show humans how to *Be.*

Animals are not beneath us, nor are they to be used for entertainment. They are, as you will read, our precious guides, guards, and guardians.

Animals appear in our lives to guide us in becoming better, more compassionate, loving beings. When they cross our paths, they attempt to share wisdom that will awaken us to our higher selves, which is exactly what the animals in this chapter speak.

If you have a fur baby who has crossed over, may you come to know through these experiences, they are still present, sharing their unadulterated wisdom and miraculous ability to help you through life.

## Heartbeat of Home

While in meditation one night, I asked the divine, if it were in alignment, to show me the afterlife dimension where I would dwell after I leave the body.

I was taken on a visual journey to a woodland forest filled with large rocks, waterfalls, caves, and streams. Magical iridescent lights glowed amidst a blue, sparkling sky.

I saw myself standing on a rock looking out across the land, knowing this was my home. I recognized that only animals and nature existed there.

I spoke with the divine light and enjoyed the majestic beauty surrounding me. Then I heard the light speak, saying, *"The beings who dwell here are you and all the animals you have met and helped while on Earth."*

I then noticed a large ancient tree standing in the center. The sky was sparkling green and shining brightly. Then a golden light glowed behind the ancient tree.

The tree's limbs began growing outward, casting a deep shadow over the ground. The golden light faded, and the scene mysteriously darkened.

I wondered and worried why the darkness came in. So, I spoke with the divine light again. As I did, I noticed the light and beautiful scene returned.

I then saw myself sitting at the edge of a beautiful lake, surrounded by waterfalls, wading my feet in the water.

I realized that worrying brings darkness yet, speaking with the divine light brings *the light.*

Next, a bird of paradise flew in, just to the right of me. It was very bright and colorful, with a triangle-shaped head. Then a giant grasshopper walked up to my left. It was a brilliant green, and it, too, had a *triangular* head.

They both looked at me and knew me, and I knew them. I knew we had been together throughout eternity. I received their message: the triangle represents *the trinity of me, it, and them.*

Lying on my bed, I returned from my journey to the present time, and as I did, I felt a heart beating on my knee. My knee was also warm. Curiously, I moved it to see if the heartbeat would subside. *It did not.*

My dog, Dakota, then jumped on the bed and quickly halted. He looked down at my knee and walked around it as if to avoid something lying there.

He laid down facing my knee and cocked his head side to side as if he were listening to someone speak. I sensed that one of my jungle friends had come back with me and was lying over my knee.

After a few minutes, I said, *"Alrighty then!" Me, it,* and *Dakota* all fell fast asleep together.

While I could not see who was on my knee, *my dog did.* When I returned from my journey vision I knew, *"It is the light of animals that shows us the true meaning of divine love."* I also learned a valuable life lesson: *no matter what happens in life, worrying brings darkness, and speaking with the divine brings the light.* Our only duty as human beings is to learn from both animals and the light.

From that moment on, I have understood the language of animals.

## Animal Talk

I communicate with animals *soul-to-soul* through telepathic energy-based transmission. Typically, that takes place in my waking state of awareness. However, the following experience took me to the *depths* of expanded consciousness.

When I sleep, I often travel out of body, experiencing other dimensions of consciousness. Every living thing does this when they sleep.

There was a time when I was speaking various animal languages when I slept. My fiancé repeatedly woke me up, either laughing or freaking out, telling me I was *"speaking animal again."*

He had often nudged me to wake, stating I had been barking and whining like dogs, ribbiting like frogs, chucking like a panther, or cawing like a crow.

One morning, he woke me up with a look of utter surprise on his face. He said he had been sitting there listening to me speak whale! *"You were making sonar sounds just like a whale! How the heck do you do these things?"* He asked.

I was just as surprised as he was because I've never even made a whale sound. However, I knew what he was referring to.

I recalled swimming with a pod of whales and speaking to them in their language. I was guiding the family and directing them on which way they needed to go to be safe, but I didn't know I was actually speaking.

Of course, I entertained us by trying to talk whale while awake *and couldn't - so* I just looked at him and said, *"I told you, I reeeeally love animals!"*

## Shakers

Shakers was my precious 22-year-old SilverPoint Persian cat.

When it was approaching his time to cross over, he was quite weak. I knew he was hanging on because he didn't want to leave me.

I called my friend, a healing touch practitioner, and asked if she would assist him in crossing over.

She came to the salon and spent some time with Shakers, but every time he was on the verge of crossing, he would hear my voice and perk up, looking for me. I knew he wasn't going anywhere without me.

That evening, I sat in bed with Shakers on my lap and just loved on him. I spoke soothingly with him, and he looked up at me and listened intently.

I told him his body wouldn't support him anymore, and it was okay to go home. I reassured him we would be together again when I crossed over. As soon as he understood, everything happened simultaneously.

He went limp in my arms; I heard a "pop" and watched in absolute awe as a hazy, white ball of light shot out of his little body.

The light flew across the room and hovered in the corner as if Shakers was looking at me.

My mouth dropped open. I said, *"Hi, Shaky. It's okay now. I'll be with you soon."* His soul then disappeared in mid-air.

This was my first visual experience of an animal's soul departing the body.

Shakers blessed me with the immovable fact that animals are divine light, and just like humans, they have a soul within.

Through Shakers, I became empowered to advocate for the souls of all animals, and in great honor of his teachings, I do.

## Kitten Love

My young friend, who was ten years old at the time, called me one night very upset about her kitten who had passed over.

She asked if I could speak with the kitten to see if she was okay. While talking with her on the phone, I received a vision.

I told my little friend, *"I am not sure why the bathroom is your kitten's hangout, but I see her sitting on the edge of the bathtub with you when you are taking a bath."*

I reassured her that she didn't need to worry about her kitten because she was *not dead, gone, or alone.*

My little friend was so comforted.

She then said, *"Oh, I bet she is in the bathroom with me because we buried her right outside the bathroom window."*

## Raccoon Tears

As much as the subject upsets me, I am led to include this experience to awaken people to the trauma animals endure when they are murdered.

A friend of mine asked me to do an energy cleansing on her home. Her husband was a hunter and had placed stuffed and mounted animals throughout the house.

She could feel the heavy energy of death in the house, and when I entered, I felt it too.

I went to each animal that had been murdered and stuffed. I apologized for the harm mankind had done, prayed for their peace, and sent them love.

I was led downstairs to a specific room. Although I saw no animals in the room, I *heard* an animal screaming in terror.

I left the room immediately with tears in my eyes, and I couldn't breathe.

I had to go outside to gather myself. My friend was genuinely concerned when she saw my reaction and asked me what had happened.

I told her with tears in my eyes, *"I heard a small animal screaming in pure fear. It was so scared, and it felt like it was being tortured. It sounded like a raccoon, but I didn't see any dead animals in the room."*

*"Jen,"* she said, *"there is a stuffed raccoon in the closet of that room."*

I became so angry.

I immediately communicated with the raccoon and prayed, sending the raccoon every ounce of love and compassion I had in me.

Exhausted from heartache, I went home to recuperate. I continued praying for the raccoon's tormented energy to be dissolved. I prayed the same for all animals who have been harmed by mankind.

This is one of many times I have received strong signals of the trauma animals experience. There are no words to describe the torment and fear they feel when it is happening.

All living things are spiritual beings with a divine purpose. I know many people have no problem killing animals, insects, and rodents, but every living thing *feels* what is done to it. If something moves and breathes, it feels.

No life wants to be harmed, tormented, or murdered. No matter the size, all living things seek and deserve only love, kindness, and respect for their life purpose.

To understand this statement better, you can refer to the biblical tale of *Balaam's Donkey*, wherein God's Angel spoke through the donkey, condemning the man for hitting the animal.

The story goes that when the donkey saw God's Angel standing in the road, it turned off into a field.

Angrily, Balaam beat the donkey. This happened three times.

Then the Lord opened Balaam's eyes, and he saw the Angel in the road with his sword drawn. So Balaam bowed and fell facedown.

The Angel asked him, "*Why have you beaten the donkey? I have come here to oppose you because your path is a reckless one.*

*The donkey saw me.*

*If it had not turned away, I would have killed you by now.*"

Humans cannot know anything about any living thing unless we are willing to communicate lovingly with its spirit.

Remember, Animals see what we can't and know what we don't.

You never know. The next animal or insect you kill may have been a divine messenger or a loved one in spirit.

# Mr. Furb

**M**y Mr. Furb was Shaker's son. He was a very regal Smokey Silver-Point Persian with a gentle soul.

We had been through a lot together. At sixteen years old, he had a major stroke. He couldn't eat, walk, drink, or stand up.

Everyone thought I should end his life. I, however, resolved that we don't kill people when they have a stroke, so why kill animals when they have one?

Honoring that consciousness, I asked Mr. Furb if he wanted to stay here or go home to the beyond. I told him if he did want to stay, he would have to help me and work hard at rehabilitation.

He transmitted agreement, and our journey of rehabilitation began.

It took four hardworking months of 24/7 effort, but Mr. Furb did it. My little guy stood happy, fully functioning, and a miracle in the doctor's eyes.

Interestingly, after his recovery, he had acquired a special little friend *in a white silk flower.*

He would carry that flower in his mouth all around the house. He would drop it on the floor and start talking to it. He even slept with it. I knew it wasn't the actual flower he adored but rather the spirit he saw in it.

At the age of 20, Mr. Furb was ready for the other side. He was barely hanging on. I held him, his little paw gripping my finger, and told him that it was okay to go home to our afterlife paradise and that his whole family would be there.

I said, *"Your daddy, Shakers, will meet you, and one day we will all be together again."*

He understood. As I stroked his head and sang a little love song to him, he stopped grasping my finger. I kissed him and prayed for the divine to bless his travels home to his family.

Just as Mr. Furb took his last breath, I saw and felt the power of his soul move into my hand, through my body, and down my legs. The wave of his soul moving through me knocked me backward, and I felt as if I were going to pass out.

I had never experienced a soul move through me before, so I felt infinitely blessed to have experienced him that way.

I knew he left his light within me. That light turned out to be the gift of being able to see him on the other side.

A few days later, when I was in meditation, Mr. Furb came to visit me. He showed me a vision of him sitting upon a large rock in our afterlife paradise.

He was young, healthy, and full of joy - And lying right in front of him on the rock, was *his little friend, the white flower.*

My heart was so filled with love - for them both! I just smiled and listened to his message.

When he spoke, it was different from how other animals had transmitted. He communicated telepathically but in *human language.*

He conveyed he was good and happy, and he really liked our afterlife place. He thanked me and was incredibly happy to be there with the rest of his family.

Then, with a warm heart, I watched him jump down from the rock and bound into the forest to run and play with the other animals.

Later that evening, in meditation, Mr. Furb appeared to me again. I watched him run and jump up on the rock again. As he looked at me, I noticed his white flower was also on the rock.

He transmitted, *"This is my very own special rock, and she (speaking of the flower) stays with me at all times."*

He then showed me all the animals in our afterlife paradise. All were encircled behind him.

He transmitted, *"They all came to show you they are here waiting for you."*

Then he jumped off the rock and began running through the woods playing with the other animals. I heard him joyfully say, *"Weeee,"* just like a child does.

I laughed and was filled with joy watching him enjoy his whole and perfect life.

## The Flower

When one of my fur babies crosses over, I strip the house the day they pass. I clean, shampoo carpets, and take personal bedding and toys to the trash.

I do this so my other animals can understand that their family member has transitioned from physical to spiritual presence.

I performed this process when Mr. Furb passed over. As much as I hated to do it, I threw his precious white silk flower away.

Well, Mr. Furb let me know he clearly *disapproved* of my throwing out his flower.

When I woke up the next morning, there lay his white silk flower on the floor at my bedroom door.

The flower stayed around for about two days and then disappeared.

**More signs**

When I showered, I used to hand-feed Mr. Furb in the bathroom so the dogs wouldn't bother him. At times, I still smell his scent when I am showering.

Mr. Furb's sleeping spot was next to me on the bed. I would smell his kitty scent next to me, and at times, I would feel him jump on the bed. I would even see his little paw imprints on the comforter.

In meditation one night, I heard my sweet boy transmit he would return through another cat.

## Far Away

One evening, as I was just about to fall asleep, I saw four angels come toward me. I watched them take hold of me, and I felt a popping sensation. I realized the angels were separating me from my body.

I saw myself being lifted up from my bedroom and outward by these angels. I *knew* I was in my bed, but at the same time, I was able to *see myself out there* with the angels.

There were two angels on each side of me. I saw myself as a faint whitish image of energy hanging between them.

I then heard a voice in my room say, *"Woah...Woah...Woah."* My dog Kobi began barking at me in alert mode.

I opened my eyes and looked to where the voice had come from and saw nothing. However, my other dog was standing up on guard, looking at the same spot as I. He clearly heard the voice too.

Intrigued, I close my eyes and immediately went into full vision again. This time, I was floating out in the vast universe alone.

I then received understanding. I then received understanding. The voice I'd heard *was a spirit guardian, and it said, "Woah,"* because I was going too far away from the body.

I also understood how animals verbalizing through sound often save people from trouble because they can see everything we cannot.

I returned to a waking state and grabbed my dogs, thanking them for letting me know that *I wasn't losing it* and for keeping me from spiraling off into the Great Beyond!

## Ms. Furb

Sweet Ms. Furb was Mr. Furb's sister. She, too, was twenty years old when it was her time to return home.

When I asked her how she wanted to return there, I didn't receive a clear answer. So, I prayed to know what to do for her.

I was torn between taking her to the vet or letting her pass at home. I had already pulled into the vet's parking lot and left four times because I still couldn't get a solid read.

She was quite lifeless. I figured she would let me know when I took her to the vet's office.

When the nurse appeared, Ms. Furb looked at her and magically perked up. I knew she wanted to leave and didn't want to pass over there. So home we went.

The minute we walked through the door, she immediately went lifeless again and started the death process. I laid Ms. Furb by my side.

Having never been led to do this before, I grabbed my coloring book and began coloring a picture for her.

I sensed that coloring a beautiful picture for her filled with my love would carry her gently through crossing over. I spent the evening coloring with her by my side as she passed.

The following evening, her scent filled my bedroom for hours. My cat Anhara knew Ms. Furb was there. Anhara ran into the room, sniffing the air.

She jumped on the bed and went to lie down where Ms. Furb used to, but she moved around the spot as if Ms. Furb were still lying there.

Since Ms. Furb's spirit was present, I went into meditation to receive anything she wanted to share.

She showed me a vision of herself, Shakers, and Mr. Furb walking together in the woods of our afterlife place.

She transmitted that, unlike the others, she would not be coming back, but she would visit me often.

The wisdom Ms. Furb filled me with was, *just like humans*, animals have the choice after death to continue guiding us through another body or guiding us with her spirit.

## Meshach

Meshach was my friend's Golden Retriever. He went home to the Great Beyond at the age of 14.

Meshach had a habit of sleeping behind vehicles in the driveway. Everyone had to make sure he was out of the way before backing up.

For a few weeks after Meshach passed, my friend often felt his presence lying behind her car. She felt him so strongly that she would even wait for a few minutes before backing up, just to give his spirit time to move.

I, too, often saw Meshach's spirit lying behind the car and walking in the yard when I visited.

One morning, my friend said that she looked up at the crest of the hill nearby as she was enjoying her coffee. The sun was just beginning to rise, and she saw Meshach walk across the ridge, then pause.

She knew without a doubt it was Meshach, who looked like he was seven again, and he was saying goodbye.

Since that morning, my friend has not felt Meshach's presence, and I no longer see his spirit in the yard.

## Noble Hawk

I was called to a wildlife rehabilitation sanctuary to communicate with the animals and confirm their habitats were to their liking and beneficial for healing.

When I entered the hawk habitat and stood before a remarkably regal hawk, he transmitted a distinct message.

With an air of nobility and tone of how-dare-you, he transmitted, *"Spit the gum out before you speak to me."*

As he transmitted this, without a bit of hesitation, I immediately walked out of the room to spit the gum out. The clinician was quite confused, so she followed me out and asked what had happened.

I laughed and said, *"Well, that's a first! He told me to spit my gum out before I speak with him."*

She, too, laughed and said, *"Yeah, that's his personality all the time."*

When I returned, the hawk opened right up and willingly communicated with me. He also let me know that *chomping* gum while speaking is a sign of disrespect.

I reported the hawk's state of being to the clinician, saying, *"That hawk's soul is a very proper and honorable spirit.*

*Believe me, if his habitat weren't suitable, he would have no problem letting you know!"*

*"Yep, sounds just like him,"* she said.

## *Siwee*

**S**iwee was Mr. and Ms. Furb's sister. She had an extraordinary spark to her personality.

I called her my *sticky kitty* because she stuck to me like glue. She would even hang over my shoulder when I cleaned the house.

She was very persistent when she wanted to be with me and have my attention - and my left arm was hers. Every night when we went to bed, Siwee would curl up in my arm and tuck herself up against my side.

If I weren't ready to go to sleep when she was, she would paw my arm with a sassy attitude until I gave in.

Siwee was also twenty years old when she passed. When her soul departed the body, it was different from the others.

Her soul traveled in and out of the body for a while before it left. I knew her leaving wasn't going to be easy for either of us.

After her crossing, Siwee visited me daily, filling my home with her scent and meowing throughout the house.

I would often feel her lying on my leg, just as she always did when I sat on the couch. However, her true love revealed itself when it was bedtime.

Every night for about a week, I would feel her sassy spirit paw at my arm. Giving in, of course, I would open my arm and say, *"Okay. Come on, Siwee, it's bedtime."*

I would feel her warmth on my arm, hear her spirit purr and even notice her warm imprint on the bed under my arm.

I thought, why should I be upset when animals pass over? They just go invisible, but love and communication stay the same.

One evening while I was in meditation, Siwee transmitted that her soul was a spirit guard. She communicated that when she was persistent, she was trying to guard me from energies that would not have been good for me.

*"This is the duty of all animals,"* she transmitted.


The behavior of animals either guides or guards us from non-beneficial energies. After thinking back to times with my animals, I could see that truth.

## Maple and Champers

My sweet Maple was the gentlest being. Like her brothers and sisters previously mentioned, she, too, passed over at the age of twenty. She also visited often.

Like the others, her scent filled the air, and I would hear her soft, gentle meow echo through the house.

I had an incredibly unique connection with Maple. We never had to speak words. This was no different after she crossed over. I knew she would come back through another cat.

A couple of weeks after she passed over, my brother asked if I would take his cat, Champers. Of course, I agreed.

I knew intuitively that Champers was meant to spend the last of his years in peace and love with a furry family of his own.

I also felt Champers had some connection with Maple, so I asked my brother to send me a picture of his cat.

When I saw the photo, I teared up and said, *"Oh, Maple, you're coming home!"*

Champers was the *exact* clone of Maple.

When my brother brought Champers to me, the cat looked, acted, and smelled like Maple. He even had her soft and gentle meow.

But there was something else about him too. He had Mr. Furb's spirit, energy, and personality as well. The proof was in the evidence.

One day I looked over to see Champers playing with a special toy. He was playing with a *white silk flower.*

He even dropped it on the floor, talked to it, and then sat and stared at it. I just smiled and said, *"Hey, Mr. Furb!"*

For the record, I had no white silk flowers in my house for Champers/Mr. Furb to find. After about a week, the white flower disappeared.

Soon after, Champers went home to be with his furry family in the Great Beyond, and I have no doubt their precious white flower is with them.

## Invisible Friends

It seemed every time I had skeptical clients in my chair, the spirit activity increased at my salon.

People would often hear one of my spirit kitties meowing or hear the pitter-patter of tiny feet running through the salon.

One day I had a client in my chair at work. She turned to me with a confused look and asked me if I had a cat in the salon.

I responded, *"No. Why?"*

She said, *"I swear I just heard a cat meow."*

I laughed and said, "Well, I should say, I don't have a visible cat here. I do have spirit kitties, though."

She was a little creeped out but seemed to be okay with it all.

**On another occasion,** I was doing an energy session on a client.

Suddenly, she sat up, looked down at her feet, and said curiously, *"Um, I just felt something small, like a cat, jump up on the bed."*

In amazement, we both watched tiny paw prints being imprinted on the paper that lined the bed.

Thoroughly entertained, my client lay back down and smiled.

When I asked her what she was enjoying, she said, *"I can feel the cat lying by my side. It is so comforting."*

I said, *"Oh, that's my Shakers boy. He's very healing."*

Another skeptical client was present when my dog Dakota decided to play chase across the salon floor with an invisible friend.

With a look of fear, my client asked, "What is he chasing?"

*"Oh, he's just playing with his spirit friends,"* I responded.

Well, *I never saw that guy again!*

## Pup Prayer

One of my clients was distraught over a dog who had been chained up outside and neglected.

She tried everything to get the owner to set him free. The police had also been called, but they couldn't do anything to help the dog.

My client asked the man repeatedly if she could take the dog and give it a better home, and he always refused. There seemed to be no hope of setting this dog free.

When she came to see me, my client was sick and unable to sleep due to thinking about the dog constantly.

I said, "Well, it sounds like the only thing you can do now is a power-prayer."

We then talked a bit about how to power-pray, which is to pray not from hope but from the depths of pure passion knowing the prayer will become so.

The next time my client came to the salon, she said she had gone home the night we talked, lit a candle, and power prayed for the dog.

To her surprise, the very next day, the dog was *free*.

The man had given the dog to a friend of my client.

That li'l pup now has a wonderful home and lots of love, thanks to the energy of love and prayer.

## No Time

A client came in terribly upset because her daughter's cat had been diagnosed with diabetes. Both she and her daughter loved the cat more than anything.

My client said, *"I prayed and prayed, and it says in the Bible whatever is prayed with the word would be so."*

She then said her daughter took her cat to the vet, and the vet suggested that she euthanize her. She did.

My client began crying and said, *"I'm angry at God for not answering my prayers."*

She asked me why God didn't heal the cat. I explained while there may be times when an animal may need our help when suffering, this wasn't one of those times.

I told her we still need to seek higher sources and what the animal wants and shared the miracle healing of my cat Shakers after his stroke.

Then I rattled off a list, saying:

- It sounds like you prayed only speaking the words and not *"with"* the word.

- You didn't allow God an opportunity to answer your prayer.

- Your daughter didn't give the cat time to heal.

- She didn't get another opinion, and she didn't ask the cat what it wanted.

*"How can we blame God or justify being upset if we interfere?"* I then asked.

I reassured her by sharing my understanding of death, saying, *"I trust that when an animal (or anything) dies, it's their soul's time to go."*

Knowing my list of answers was probably hard to hear, I concluded, compassionately suggesting that in the future, she should seek other veterinary opinions and consult with the animal, and if she can't do that herself, call on an animal communicator.

## Dakota

My Angel, Dakota, was an Australian Shepherd, Golden Retriever cross. Dakota and I were attached in more ways than one.

Dakota was my guard, guide, and spiritual teacher. He taught me about death, the invisible worlds, and natural healing.

Dakota was *beyond* intuitive. We were psychically connected through our souls, which taught me the wisdom and ability of soul-to-soul communion.

Through my experience with Dakota, I eventually understood that the souls of animals ultimately reflect *our higher selves.*

Dakota went everywhere with me not only because it was his spiritual position but also because he was prone to having grand-mal seizures.

When he and his little brother Kobi sensed a seizure coming on, one of them would come get me to help Dakota through it. Dakota always depended on me to help him through with healing energy.

As life is, we can only last so long before the body eventually weakens. Dakota was twelve years old when the vet phoned to tell me he had diagnosed my beloved companion with cancer.

The doctor said he wouldn't live any more than two-three months. I, however, said, *"Okay. We will see."*

While I didn't know *how* I knew *nature* would be the route to take with Dakota's treatment. After hanging up with the vet, I went to Dakota and asked him what he wanted to do.

He transmitted that crossing over early was not an option, and neither was invasive treatment. He confirmed I was to take the natural route and consult with him and spirit guides on everything regarding his care. And I did.

Later that evening, as Dakota slept soundly next to me, he came to me in spirit.

He transmitted, *"I will tell you when and how I must go, and when it is time. You have to learn things before I go."*

In this vision, I saw myself vowing to care for Dakota naturally. When I woke up the next morning, I had a profound respect for him and his soul's purpose. I understood that living two-three months was *not* in the divine plan.

For the next two years, Dakota and three spirit guides taught me everything I know about the soul and natural medicine firsthand.

Every time I took him to the vet, the doctor was pleasantly surprised at how well Dakota was doing.

He knew I was treating him naturally and energetically and simply said, *"Continue what you're doing. It's working."*

The "C" word didn't stop Dakota from enjoying life and his favorite things.

The symptoms of cancer appeared to be awful, but Dakota was on a strict natural diet and holistic pain management routine that spared him from associated pain and suffering.

Surprisingly, Dakota experienced more troubling issues with his seizures than he did from cancer.

Two weeks before Dakota passed over, he was still eating, drinking, playing, and not to my liking, eating cat poo out of the litter box!

## A Brother Knows

My Chihuahua Kobi loved his brother Dakota more than anything.

They were best buddies. Kobi would even attack larger dogs if they played too roughly with Dakota. The two were attached at the hip for nearly fourteen years.

I knew Dakota's time was near when his li'l buddy Kobi woke me up one night. Kobi was sitting next to Dakota, whining with a look of pure worry and heartache. Little Kobi was in emotional agony for his best friend.

I knew that was the moment Kobi understood Dakota was going to be leaving him.

I comforted and reassured him Dakota would be okay and would visit us.

Kobi looked at me and then Dakota a few times. I knew he was trying to process what I said. I transmitted calming energy to Kobi until he fell asleep, tightly tucked up with his brother.

*Dakota crossed over four days later.*

A week before this experience, I witnessed a beautiful moment confirming Dakota's time was near.

I was watching Dakota sleeping on the floor when he lifted his head as if he had heard something. He jumped up and ran after something, which *invisibly, ran* through the sliding glass door.

He stood there for a second, looking into the glass. I knew, without a doubt, he was looking into another dimension beyond this world.

Then instantly, he was overcome with pure joy as if he saw someone he recognized through the glass. His eyes widened, and he began to wag his tail, and his whole body wiggled with joy. He was so happy recognizing a friend.

I just watched in awe, knowing that whoever he saw in that moment came to show him the way and would be there to greet him when he crossed over, and he would be very happy.

## Our Agreement

**D**akota's life purpose was to teach me that nature's medicine, divine spirit, and intuition can overcome the suffering mentality so I may teach others.

As a great functional medicine professor, he chose me as his student. I knew once I had learned all he had to teach me, he would return to the afterlife.

Dakota and I had an agreement. When it came time for his soul to leave his body, he would let me know.

This was extremely challenging because it was up to me to read and communicate perfectly to understand his wishes - *which I bombed three times.*

The first time I thought it was time for his soul's departure, I called to make the appointment with the vet. Just as I hung up the phone, I was led to look out the window.

When I did, I saw a hawk circling in the sky, which for me represents the Great Spirit/God is present.

Then, I saw an old man with a cane walking up a steep hill. This was a clear sign that Dakota wasn't ready to go, and it symbolized Dakota may have been old and in need of assistance, but he was *still walking uphill.*

I decided to keep the vet appointment just in case I wasn't intuiting correctly. While driving, I asked for one final sign to stop me if the doctor was not supposed to assist with Dakota's cross-over.

Well, my check engine light came on! *That's all I needed.*

When I opened the door to the vet's office, I told his doctor, *"I'm sorry to do this again, but I'm not supposed to do this."*

He looked at Dakota joyfully running to the treat bin and said, *"I agree. I'm not going to do it either. He's too alert."*

Dakota and I went home, and he joyfully continued teaching me.


With pure gratitude, I thanked the hawk, God, and the old man for guiding me, and I was so grateful Dakota's vet was intuitive too.

## Dying Together

I don't know where this came from, but not long after Dakota started showing signs of illness, I looked at him and said, *"It's okay, angel. You are not going through this alone. We are going to die together."*

*And we did.*

I knew the time was near when we both became sick with pneumonia. We died together for over a week.

Knowing Dakota wouldn't make it through one more day, I prayed and blessed his soul's journey, anointing him and myself with frankincense and myrrh.

Sensing the following morning was Dakota's time, I took him once more to the vet.

When the doctor left the examination room to retrieve the relaxer for Dakota, he again perked up and wanted to leave. We were shocked!

So once again, I told the doctor I just couldn't do it and that Dakota clearly wanted to pass at home with me.

I was completely stressed out with worry, and the doctor wasn't happy because Dakota was clearly at the end. I reminded the doctor that I had an agreement with Dakota that *he* would be the one telling me when the time was right.

As agonizing as it was to wait and hope he wasn't suffering, I had to honor his wishes and my soul agreement with him. I carried Dakota to the car and left.

We weren't gone from the vet's office 15 minutes before Dakota started the death process.

I knew he just wanted to be alone with me and go for one last car ride with Momma before he departed. He wouldn't have had it any other way.

I called the doctor and told him Dakota was in the death process, and I was bringing him back to ease the transition.

Knowing Dakota's process so well, the doctor quickly gave him the relaxer to ensure he would not get up and want to leave again.

I stood next to my darling Dakota, filling him with my purest love and thanking him for all he taught me. I whispered in his ear, *"Doodles, you come back to me when you can. I will see you soon, Angel."*

Just as I said that, I felt his soul leap out of his body. Like a mighty, beautiful wind, his soul went through my body, exited through my back, and flew around the room.

His soul exited before the body shut down. As I felt his soul disappear from the room, I left knowing Dakota and I would be together again soon – and in no time, we were.

Dakota returned one month later, *on my birthday no less.*

## Cat Box!

The evening Dakota passed to the Great Beyond, my electricity started to surge through the house randomly. I knew his spirit was present.

I said, *"Yay, Angel Boy, you've found your way home!"*

Dakota transmitted, *"I'm not an Angel anymore. I'm a presence."*

The next morning, he left me a mind-blowing, crystal-clear sign of his presence; *a classic reference to our lifelong battle over his getting into the cat box!*

I woke to find a chewed-up cat *"treat"* on the floor by my bedroom door!

It had Dakota's teeth marks all over it!

I laughed out loud and yelled, *"Ugh! Dakota! Really? Even in spirit?"*

I was positive he was laughing too.

## Helping Brother

I was very worried about Kobi missing his best buddy Dakota terribly. He was so depressed and had no life energy in him.

He wouldn't eat, play, or even come when I called him. He just lay in Dakota's spot on the bed. When Kobi began vomiting, I knew he wouldn't live long if the depression continued.

As I tearfully cleaned the house and packed up Dakota's things, I felt Dakota's presence enter the room and transmit, *"Stop crying, Momma, I'm coming back."*

With joy and a warm heart, I said, *"I know you are, but Kobi doesn't. He misses you so much. Please go tell Kobi and let him see you."*

Dakota transmitted, *"I will,"* and I felt his presence leave.

Ten minutes later, Kobi came running out of the bedroom full of joy, bursting with life energy.

He looked up at me as if he was saying, *"Mom, come look! Dakota's here!"*

I was so comforted, in complete awe of this miracle.

Kobi had no more upset after this glorious day. Dakota had indeed helped his little brother.

*Ask, and you shall receive.*

## A Gift for Momma

The week after Dakota's crossing-over, I was driving to work, and as I neared a landmark, I felt Dakota's presence pop in and transmit, *"Turn there. There's a gift for you."* So I did.

The minute I turned the corner, I knew exactly what he was gifting me. It was the largest maidenhair fern I had ever seen.

I knew that was the gift because of the bright light beam shining directly on the fern - and nowhere else.

Maidenhair ferns represent *new life and rebirth*.

Later that evening, while in meditation, Dakota transmitted, *"I am coming back when the fern dies. That will be the sign I am back."*

As interesting as that sounded, I knew I would just have to wait and see.

## Snoopy Dance

The very night Dakota crossed over, I was sitting in bed, and his scent filled the room.

I then heard him let out his famous *"I want"* sound.

When Dakota wanted something, he wouldn't bark. He would instead make a chucking sound like a panther.

Later that evening, while I was in meditation, Dakota showed me a vision of himself as the cartoon character Snoopy dancing on his two backlegs.

Dakota's long white hair flowed as he joyfully jumped up in the air.

He transmitted, *"I'm good. Thank you."*

I wondered if this meant he would be returning as a small white dog like Snoopy.

## New Colors

I began receiving visions from Dakota regarding the appearance of the dog he would be integrated with.

He showed me a vision of a Bernese Mountain Dog and transmitted, *"Kobi will know him when he sees the dog. You will know by Kobi's love for me."*

He then showed me a vision of Kobi jumping up and hugging the new dog around the neck, the same way he used to do with Dakota.

Assuming this meant Dakota was going to come back in a Bernese Mountain Dog, I said, *"Dakota, li'l dude, can't you pick something smaller? Remember, we have a one-bedroom apartment here!"*

Six days after Dakota crossed over, I had a vision while I slept of Dakota speaking to me.

He transmitted, *"When the clock strikes three, you will know it's me."*

I understood this message to mean - at three o'clock, I would know which dog he would return as.

*I noticed the maidenhair fern began to die out.*

## The Mysterious Voice

Even with Dakota showing me visions and a message of him returning through another dog, I was still quite reluctant to get another one.

I had been drawn to a particular dog at the humane society, but I felt Kobi should have all the attention for a while, so I did not go meet this dog.

While at work, I heard a spirit transmit, *"Go to the shelter now."*

I pondered the thought for a moment and chose to ignore the guidance. Then I heard the spirit say again, and this time with some attitude, *"Go now!"*

So, I grabbed Kobi and left for the shelter.

When I met this dog named Chase at the shelter, I could feel Dakota's energy, but I didn't sense his presence in Chase.

Honestly, I didn't feel this dog was the one, which is probably why Dakota wanted Kobi to have the final say. *Ha-ha*. But, I honored Dakota's guidance and brought Kobi in to meet Chase.

Of course, Chase was hyper from being caged, and Kobi can be cocky, so I held Kobi while they met.

Kobi growled at Chase, and it appeared he didn't like him. Just as I felt it was time to go, I heard spirit transmit, *"Put Kobi down. He can't show you the truth if you hold him."*

I immediately put Kobi on the kennel floor. Kobi ran over to Chase, sniffed him up and down, and then, as if he were hit with an awakening, Kobi started joyfully whining, jumped up, and hugged Chase the same way he used to embrace Dakota.

To my comfort and amazement, just as Dakota said, I signed the papers to take Chase/Dakota home - *when the clock struck 3:00 p.m.*

I, of course, changed Chase/Dakota's name appropriately to Howakhan, which means *"Of the mysterious voice."*

Just as Dakota had shown me, Howakhan has Bernese Mountain Dog's colors on his face, white flowing hair, and he often dances just like Snoopy on his two back legs!

And thankfully, he's half the size of a Bernese Mountain Dog.

Kobi got his brother back.

Dakota got his family back.

Chase/Howakhan has an exciting new life.

And, I have an eclectic, amazing new teacher.

## I Know My Way

When I brought *Chase/Dakota/Howakhan* home from the shelter, the minute I shut the car door, he knew exactly where to go.

Having three buildings of choice, he instantly turned toward my condo, knowing that was the building we call home.

He started running, dragging me up the stairs leading me directly to our condo. He knew to turn right at the top of the stairs - and he led me straight to our front door.

He knew everything about his home.

When we entered the condo, he ran up to the cats and kissed them, his tail wagging as if he were saying, *"Hey, I'm back. I've missed you."*

Chase/Dakota/Howakhan also knew our routine, timing, and how and where I fed the dogs.

*The next day, the Maidenhair Fern died.*

## Two for One

**H**owakhan has every one of Dakota's traits, and believe me, Dakota did not have *ordinary* characteristics.

I had the pure joy of watching two dogs exist in one body. Some days he is Chase/Howakhan, and other days, he is Dakota.

Dakota spent his entire life going to work with me every day. He had been around my clients and friends for almost 14 years.

When my clients and friends met Howakhan, they all said, "That's definitely Dakota!"

Out of sheer habit, it was hard for everyone not to call him Dakota. But it didn't matter. Every time we slipped and called him Dakota, he would come running.

I thought I would play with this and test Howakhan by calling him Dakota's nicknames, such as *Doodles, Angel Boy, Roo, Buddy, and Lovie.* Howakhan came running every time I called out any one of those names.

Everyone knew Dakota was back - *including the maidenhair fern.*


One evening in meditation, I received a confirming vision. I was shown Dakota and Chase/Howakhan agreeing they would share time in the same body for a while.

Then, at a divinely specific time, one would choose to stay in the body, and the other would remain in spirit. Either way, I am beyond blessed to enjoy life with so many amazing spirits!

## Karma and Dharma

My sweet Dakota had such a carefree spirit, and he didn't have a mean bone in his body. He loved all animals. I even found him loving on a dead mouse one day, gently trying to bring it back to life.

Collie breeds, however, didn't like him one bit. Every time a collie laid eyes on Dakota, it would attack him. It was such a common occurrence that I would have to leave dog parks to keep Dakota safe.

I used to tell him if he ever reincarnated here, he'd better choose to be a collie so they would quit picking on him.

Dakota was so full of love, but he wasn't a big kisser. I might get one quick kiss every six months or so.

I often told him, *"Next time you come back to me, you better be a dog who loves kissing!"*

Well, Dakota brought karma to collies and dharma to me.

Howakhan happens to be a collie! He is a rare Border Collie and Smooth Collie breed. And just as I thought, collies no longer attack him.

As for Dakota's lack in the kissing department, well, Howakhan kisses so much I can't complete a task without having to stop to receive his kisses.

If you let him, he would seriously kiss you for hours. Even when I am driving the car, he comes to the front to check on me every five minutes and lays a bunch of kisses on my cheek.

I have no doubt Dakota understood every word I said when I told him to come back as a big-kissing collie!

## Angels are Sweet

I was waiting for Dakota to lead me to the perfect time and place to spread his ashes.

About a year after he crossed over, I jumped out of bed one morning, knowing that was the day to scatter the ashes of his old body, and I knew exactly where we were going.

Dakota and Kobi loved Mount Mitchell to receive electro-magnetic energy from the four directions. That is where Dakota led me to return his ashes to the universe as energy, and with the autumnal equinox/full-moon alignment on this day, it was the perfect time and place.

The "Mitchell" theme also held a heart-string meaning with Dakota. Dakota's favorite person in the world was Mitchell. He loved Mitchell so much I would have to give Dakota a valium before Mitchell visited so he wouldn't have a seizure from the excitement.

Interestingly, while driving to Mt. Mitchell, I received a vision. I saw myself spreading the ashes, and a wind came in and blew Dakota's ashes into my face and mouth.

That actually happened the last time I went with a friend to spread the ashes of her mother. Not only did her ashes smell like death, but they tasted like death too. I couldn't get that awful taste out of my mouth for two days. I surely didn't want it to happen again!

As I began hiking up to the mount's summit, Dakota led me to notice a trail. I knew that was the place.

After spending some time at the summit receiving energy, just like we always did, I returned to the trail.

I first made sure there was no wind blowing. Then I opened the bag and said a prayer.

Just as I started to toss the ashes, a colossal wind blew in, blowing the ashes right in my face, mouth, and all over me! I busted out laughing - knowing I should have expected that!

As I was spitting out the ashes, I laughed pleasantly surprised as I realized that Dakota's ashes smelled and tasted sweet, unlike the human body. There was no foulness at all.

I just smiled with a warm heart, knowing he was still teaching me through my experiences - as he confirmed what I had always known... *Animals are sweet, divine messengers.*

As I turned to go home, I realized a powerful message, *"No matter what form of being a soul takes, visible or invisible - everyone and everything is still infinitely alive, present, and always accessible."*

Life IS death, and Death IS life.

*One way of life we can see, hear and touch.*

*The other must be sensed, known, and trusted.*

## Afterlife Thoughts

The concept of humans thinking they need to survive is an elusive perception because the soul's consciousness is limitless.

*We will not live in the body forever because we don't need to. We live infinitely.*

Death is not ever the end of our existence. Bodily death is just our rebirth into the original creation of ourselves. When we return to the Great Beyond, we merely move, exist in a different location, with a new position, just like we do in the earthly life.

However, the stress we endure on Earth stays there. When we leave the body and enter the beyond, it is familiar. We know that life is our home, and every being there knows us.

While life and death *appear* to be two separate events, they are not. Because every living thing has a soul, all life exists as both a materialized and infinite being, and simultaneously omnipresent: *here, there, and everywhere.*

We can acknowledge this miraculous part of our design through the countless people all over the world who have experienced the afterlife directly.

Although born perfect and whole, we have all been taught by humankind to become dual beings. Bodily death corrects those teachings by rebirthing us to our perfect invisible form.

In that state of our being, we remember our cohesive, omnipresent relationship between creation and creator itself. Therein, all living things are descendants - omnipresent, infinite souls of the glorious mystery.

How a person or pet dies often hits people hard, mentally.

Unfortunately, we don't get to choose how and when we or others die. The divine creation has made it so we do not interfere with sacred process of the soul - or its destiny.

When one departs the body and returns home to the afterlife, that day, date, time, and how the body dies were encoded within the cells prior to birth.

When it appears a person or a pet is suffering, they are likely not. The soul-mind has what I call a *detach button* where the soul escapes the body before a trauma. In my experiences, when the soul, the *supreme sensory self,* has exited the body vessel, the ego consciousness supporting pain and suffering ceases. Therein, pain is not felt.

What looks like pain and suffering to an onlooker is merely the brain reacting from memory and the body mechanically responding to the soul's departure.

What we witness at death is an illusion because we cannot see the soul and invisible divine forces assisting the being in that moment.

Death is only hard to deal with because we have been *trained* to believe in the ideas of separation, loss, pain, and suffering.

Humankind is so focused on making death traumatizing, they forget about the perfect living spirit. If we look beyond that fabrication and remember the soul exits before the human body dies, we can easily continue loving relationships with our loved ones.

Death is not a surprise event. Every living thing begins the death process the moment it takes its first breath in this world. Death is a process of life.

And still, most humans spend their entire lifetime trying to avoid death and treat it like it's a terrible surprise and not supposed to happen.

Life is not based on birth and death. Life and death are one continuous, evolving rebirth of our infinite consciousness. In this, and with all of the experiences I've shared from beyond, we can genuinely conclude that life and our relationships with loved ones do not end.

Our loved ones in spirit are perfect as unadulterated guardians. Their greatest gift is that they can love and guide us in a way they could not in the body.

Every experience you have is a precious moment where divine beings are trying to guide you through life. May you always remember your loved ones, pets, and the divine, though invisible, are not gone. They want us to stay connected with them and continue receiving their love and guidance.

After all, that is why they return to their spirit self... *to help prepare us for our own return to the Life Beyond Us.*

## Playtime

As a way for your loved ones to bring a personal message to you from the other side, you may enjoy doing a word search with all the large print letters within the book.

```
I M W M T T M A T N N W I F I M A M M T A M N
A M I M I I O I I O W A I I O O A A A F M A T O
T I A W A I D A M O T I A I O A I I M F M J P L T
M W M W O T O T I M I T I O W S O D T W C W S
D T O W W A T T I W I S M A M W O S M I S M I
    O A M M D I T I T T I E W H M I
```

Find as many words as you can in the jumble. Then take those words and arrange a sentence or statement.

You just might end up with an exquisite enlightening message from a loved one in the Life Beyond Us!

## Remember your loved ones who have crossed over.

Take a moment to speak to the divine and your loved ones who have crossed. Thank them for loving you and for being your guides, guards, and guardians by writing their names or a special note to them on this page.

## Other Books By Jennifer A. Bryant

**Life Beyond Us** - *An eclectic, mind-blowing memoir of heartwarming and mysterious spiritual experiences with the afterlife.*

**Woodland Angels** - *A comforting, magical life guide for children and adults helping to see life challenges in other ways.*

**Infinite Wellness** - *An all encompassing wellness guide based on natural living and functional wellness for the body, mind, and spirit.*

**Emerge** - *An eye-opening self-help practice guide to overcome self-undoing limitations.*

**Fur Babies Speak** - *A heart-warming journal of signs and mysteries shared with my pets in the great beyond.*

**The Garden** - *An inspiring handbook of quotes reflecting life thoughts to ponder for higher consciousness.*

Jennifer Bryant

*https://jenniferbryantholisticwriter.wordpress.com*

## Thy Story, Thy Song

This is the story,

Thy spirit ~ Eternal...

free as love and everything ~

in every space.

Invisible to mortal eyes.

Yet -

One with all manifestations.

Then, passing through ~

the infinite veil of gravity...

The soul inhabits a materialized vessel,

As Thy story -

manifesting experience ~

Temporarily.

Yet, Thy song...

is Rebirth ~

thy Spirit Eternal,

Freed to return As Love ~ with the All,

As thy perfect spirit,

Eternal and Indestructible.

Life is never taken away...

As it has never been had, to have been taken.

Life and loved one's merely change form ~

as part of the divine, infinite experience.

Rebirth is the process.

Not a destination.

All living - All grace-filled.

All still alive as Spirit.

Within you and beyond you...

Love continues ~

Only in a different way.

The Spiritual continuum lives on...

boundless and infinitely aware.


Always guiding us through the story of our Song:

Which began first -

in the Life Beyond Us...

Made in the USA
Columbia, SC
24 December 2021